Shobhaa Dé

S's Secret...

PopulaR prakashan

www.popularprakashan.com

Popular Prakashan Pvt. Ltd.
301, Mahalaxmi Chambers
22, Bhulabhai Desai Road, Mumbai - 400026.

© December 2009, Shobhaa Dé
First Reprint : December 2009

ISBN - 978-81-7991-438-0
(4186)

Cover design: Subhash Awchat
Author Photograph: Vikram Bawa
Illustrations: Omkar Nerlekar

Printed in India
by Thomson Press (India) Ltd.
B-315, Okhla Phase-I
New Delhi

Published by
Ramdas Bhatkal
for Popular Prakashan Pvt. Ltd.
301, Mahalaxmi Chambers
22, Bhulabhai Desai Road
Mumbai - 400026.

To

Children of all ages -
the best story-tellers
in the world...

From the Author...

What would life be without children? I can hear countless harried moms saying, "Blissful!"

But.... boring!! Right, moms??

So, this one is for you...for putting up with, well, what mothers the world over put up with 24x7... I guess I don't need to spell it out!

And this is for you too, kids! Go ahead... give us a hard time. Someday you'll be parents... and then we'll talk!

Thanks Harsha and Team Popular Prakashan. This is a first for me, and I sure as hell needed that hand-holding.

Finally, thanks Subhash Awchat for designing the cover. I love the jacket... so will our young readers.

'S's Secret' has been so much fun to write - now go discover what the secret is!

Enjoy the book.

Shobha Dé

Chapter One

No Cakewalk

"Have you told Mom, yet?" Pia's voice was low and anxious. Sandhya shook her head and continued to whisk the sticky mixture of flour and butter in the neat kitchen, which was the centre of the Mehta home.

"How can you bake a cake when you know Mom will be angry? Or are you planning not to tell her at all?" Pia persisted.

Sandhya looked at her younger sister sharply and placed a finger on her own lips. "Sssh... Bhaiya will hear... don't say anything... please, please... just keep quiet till Bhaiya leaves... he's late for college again."

Just then, Siddhartha a tall, athletic eighteen-year-old rushed into the kitchen. "Where's my skimmed milk... Oh man... I'm late for eco... and the toast is burnt as usual. Sandhya... don't just stand there with that stupid expression... make me a sandwich... fast... Tell Mom I am going straight to Subi's place for stats tuitions. And you... little monkey... go wash your hands... filthy as always."

The two girls looked at their brother, then at each other. "Bhaiya, why don't you wake up on time? Don't tell us you have broken the alarm clock again?" Pia piped up.

Sid opened the fridge and made disapproving noises. "Vegetables, vegetables, vegetables – who eats all this rubbish, huh? Who? Look at all this... *bhindi, karela, palak, kadoo*. Hey you Motu, stay away from those chips... tell Mom to organise a decent dinner... What amazing food we have at Subi's... fantastic *pav-bhaji*, nachos... how come we don't have stuff like that here? His mom is like the best cook in the world. Her crab curry! Oh my God! Sandhya ... stop making those silly cakes, make some real food for a change; learn some deadly stuff… like... ok… anything deadly... ok I'm off. Send my tennis gear to the club later... behave yourselves till Mom gets home."

With that, Sid was gone. Pia rushed into her brother's room. "I knew it," she shouted triumphantly, "now wait till Dad gets home."

Sandhya left the kitchen to check what Pia was talking about. She'd half-guessed anyway. "Broken?" she enquired.

Pia giggled, "Of course... into twenty pieces; this is the sixth one... by next term, Bhaiya will have thrown ten clocks at the wall. Mom will be furious... first your... your... problem... then Bhaiya's clock. God! I hope I'm not around, or I'll also get it in the neck for nothing."

Sandhya turned angrily to her kid sister. "Listen you... stop behaving like my grandmother. Don't forget you are only nine years old... five years younger than me and nine years younger than Bhaiya. Just mind your own business, okay? I'll deal with Mom."

Pia piped up once again. "And Dad?"

"Mom will deal with him...you just stay out of this," Sandhya snapped.

"Okay, Didi, but remember you were rude to me – very rude – when I was only trying to help. Next time you're in trouble, don't come to me."

Pia sulked. Sandhya continued to whisk the flour and butter mixture mechanically. Her brow was knitted. Her frown was deeper than usual. She reasoned that Mom would be angry for sure, but she'd make it up to her somehow. As she was telling herself this, Gauritai, the faithful domestic help, walked into the kitchen with a bucketful of washed clothes. "Baby...," she started saying, as Sandhya's eyes dilated with horror.

"Oh no, Gauritai, you've done it again! That was my favourite T-shirt. I need it all the time for my badminton classes. What have you done?"

Gauritai was holding up what looked suspiciously like a pink batik top. "Pia's shorts... the red ones... colour ran. Not my fault, baby. I've told Pia a hundred times not to mix up all the clothes."

Sandhya placed the cake mix on the kitchen counter and left the room in tears.

"Not fair... not fair... my worst day... first... first that other problem in school... now this. Mom's going to kill me today."

Sandhya ran straight into the bedroom she shared with Pia, and shut the door. She knew it wouldn't be long before Pia came knocking, pretending to need something superfluous, like a hair band, when all she wanted was to watch her older sister cry and maybe, with some luck, be able to eavesdrop on her conversation on the phone. There were times when she just hated her kid sister. And this was definitely one of them.

"Go away," Sandhya sobbed, when the familiar knocking began. "I want to be alone... just leave me to myself... go... play with your stupid dolls..." The knocking didn't stop. Sandhya screamed, "Stop that... you hear me? Get lost."

"Sandhya darling... It's me... Mom... what's wrong? Just open the door."

Sandhya froze. Oh God! What was Mom doing at home? She was supposed to be at the hospital OPD (Out Patients' Department) till at least 4 p.m. Sandhya panicked and rushed to her desk. Hastily, very hastily, she picked up her schoolbag and hid it under the heavy bedcovers that were already bulging with Pia's unwashed jeans that Mom was not supposed to see.

"One sec, Mom... just changing," Sandhya fibbed, as she took one final look around the mess, wiped her tears, inspected her face for tell-tale streaks, adjusted her expression and opened the door for Mom.

"Hey... You're looking great!" Sandhya exclaimed, taking in her mother's bright orange saree, with coral accessories to match. "Mom, I really feel you should wear sarees more often."

Anuradha, Sandhya's mother, walked into the children's room and looked critically at herself in the full-length mirror. "Your father gave me this saree last year. Remember? After his trip to Chennai... yes, it's beautiful, but you know Sandhya, sarees are a little impractical on my OPD days."

Sandhya kept staring at her mother.

"You look like a real *Devi* when you wear a saree... really, Mom, you should stick to sarees. You look best in them, even Dad says so... I mean, not that you look bad in a salwar-kameez... but... but... in a saree you look amazing."

Anuradha smiled and hugged her daughter. These were the small moments she cherished in their busy lives. Sandhya was still and quiet, with her arms wrapped around her mother's narrow waist. Anu caught sight of the two of them in the mirror and gently released Sandhya.

"Gosh... You've grown taller in just two months... have you been doing those stretching exercises regularly like Dad keeps reminding you to?"

Sandhya stared guiltily at the bar covered with soft towelling that had been installed in the door frame.

Her father Dev was fond of saying, "I'd like my girls to be at least 5'8" tall... no reason why they shouldn't make it... stretch, stretch, stretch... hang from the bar twice a day... swim... these are the years... another four inches at least, that's my target."

Sandhya shook her head and confessed sheepishly that she'd forgotten all about her promise.

"I'll start again during the holidays, but please don't mention it during dinner or Dad will nag and nag."

Anu laughed and took a quick look at the room. "Hmmm... and what are you hiding under the bedcovers? Looks like a mini-mountain of dirty clothes."

Sandhya threw herself on the bed and said, "Nothing Mom... it's just some stuff, you know, Pia's shorts and things."

Anu walked up briskly to the bed. "Come on, get up, let me see... I keep telling Gauritai to collect used clothes and throw them into the washing machine... I've given you girls a large basket for sweaty clothes; why don't you use it? Here... help me tidy up."

Sandhya thought she'd distract her mother, before 'that' question was asked.

"Mom… I've just learnt a new noodle dish from Asavari. Shall I make it for dinner?"

Anu smiled indulgently at her daughter. "First, a cake. Now, noodles… You seem to be in a really obliging mood today. Tell me, have you fought with Pia again? Lost something? Come on… I know you."

Sandhya feigned hurt and pretended to sulk. "Mom, don't be mean, why would I do something like that? I just feel like making something for dinner. And Bhaiya is always so hungry."

Anu sat down on the children's twin bed and looked at their bookshelf. "Sandhya… you'd promised to tidy up your shelves and cupboard over the weekend… look at this mess."

Sandhya grumbled. "You never say anything to Pia… It's always me you're after. Even Bhaiya keeps scolding me; he never scolds Pia. Most of the mess is made by her. See those old puzzle books and see… look there… that lot was given to her on her fifth birthday. She won't let me touch it. That's why I keep saying please, please, let me have my own room. I don't mind if you make some space for me next to the drawing

8

room... but I hate sharing with Pia. She's a pig."

Anu stopped Sandhya by putting a finger on her lips. "Don't say that about your sister; she's younger than you. Set an example and she'll automatically follow. Don't call her a pig, that's so rude."

Sandhya exclaimed, "Rude? Have you ever corrected Pia? Have you heard the way she speaks to me? She calls me a donkey ten times a day. I never complain to you. She's even cheeky with Bhaiya and his friends. Nobody tells Pia anything because she's 'so-o-o-o young...' I hate her, and nothing can change that."

Anu started picking up clothes left on the floor and putting away files, books, socks, shoes. "Pia is at an age when she wants to be with you and your friends. She doesn't like being treated like a pesky kid, that's all. Speak to her with some respect yourself, and then see the difference."

"Never!" said Sandhya emphatically. "She doesn't deserve any respect. She's always interfering in my life and carrying tales to you and Dad. I want a room of my own; please Ma... I'm... grown up now. I need my own space. There's no privacy at all. Pia bugs me all the time. If we had our rooms, we wouldn't fight so much. Please tell Dad."

Anu signalled to Sandhya to sit down beside her. "Listen darling, it's not possible at this stage to give you your own room. This is our home and you have to learn to share this space with your sister. Do you know when I was growing up, I shared my room with not one but two sisters? And we didn't fight like you do."

Sandhya bit her lips to keep the tears from spilling out of her eyes. "All of you blame me as if it's my fault and Pia is an angel. If you only knew what she's up to, you wouldn't think she's so innocent and sweet... but I won't sneak on her; I'm not like that... I know lots of things that Dad and you don't know."

Anu pretended to be busy folding T-shirts. She kept her voice casual and light, as she asked softly, "What sort of things, darling? If it's something wrong Pia is doing, you should definitely tell us. Surely, you don't want her to get into serious trouble that her family doesn't know anything about? Come on, Sandhya, tell me... what is Pia doing that upsets you?"

Sandhya thought quickly, very quickly, before replying, "Mom, it isn't anything like that, don't worry. Nothing major. She... she... just does silly things that get her into trouble. Mainly she fibs a lot. And makes up stories. Do you think I wouldn't have told you or Bhaiya had it been serious? Relax. Chill. I'm handling it ... I should never have told you. Now you'll go and ask her and she'll fight with me again."

Anu turned around to face Sandhya. "I trust you. And don't worry, I won't ask. Okay? Now, come on, make the noodles... I'm starving."

Sandhya wished her mother wouldn't be so nice to her. Not today, at any rate. Nice and trusting. It made it even more difficult for Sandhya. She thought of her friends' moms. Some of them had jobs or businesses. But most were just full-time moms, always at home, always fussing and fussing. Her own mother, Anu, was a doctor. Sandhya liked that. Even if it meant less time with her. Sandhya was proud of her parents. Even her 'strict father', Dev, a busy chartered accountant. They were good parents, Sandhya reasoned, even if, at times, they behaved weirdly.

Sandhya liked her grandparents, too. Mom's mother in particular. She was cool. Really, really cool, unlike the grandmoms of some of her friends. Nani was also a doctor, though unlike her mom, who was a paediatric surgeon, Nani was an ENT surgeon.

And yes, Nani wore jeans on weekends. How cool was that? Mom used to feel a little embarrassed in the old days, when Nani came over to meet the kids. Especially since Dad's parents were more traditional and formal. Sandhya liked her dada but was not very fond of her strict dadi. Though they were kind and comforting in their own way. And Dad really looked forward to their visits.

It was Pia who was thoroughly spoilt by both sets of grandparents but that was because she always acted like a baby in their presence and behaved in an irritatingly cute way. Naturally, Bhaiya was everybody's *ladla*, but Sandhya didn't mind at all. She knew she had a special equation with them. Besides, they loved her cakes and cookies. And some of the recipes shared by her two grandmoms were so yummy, Sandhya had made her own little cookbook with them.

Mom didn't enjoy spending time in the kitchen at all. But Dad did. In fact, Dad and she loved cooking together on Sundays, trading little secrets and experimenting with new dishes. Dad said he found cooking most relaxing – it was his way of unwinding on weekends. Bhaiya, of course, loved to hog. He could eat one full meal and be ready to start again an hour later.

As for that brat Pia, all she did was crib and criticise; perhaps she felt jealous of Sandhya's expertise in the kitchen. She gobbled everything up and then started her nonsense. "Too much salt... Oof... I want to vomit. Horrible taste... Gauritai... I'm starving... I hope there's some proper food in this house... not all the rubbish I've been served just now... please give it to Zorro... No, don't, even Zorro won't eat it, ugh. Yuck... make some toast... or I'll phone for a pizza... Make real food na. My friends eat amazing snacks all day long – hamburgers and wraps. What do we eat? *Dosas, idlis, vadas...* pleeeease... we are sick of it. Learn new fancy dishes, no. We'll tell Mom to send you for cooking classes. Mrs. Talreja teaches Mexican, Chinese, French, Italian… forget *bhajiyas* and *laddoos*, give us some foreign-type food now."

In the beginning, Pia's remarks used to hurt Sandhya. There were times when she would burst into tears at the table or throw her napkin down in anger. Then, one day, Dad explained to her that Pia was only expressing her envy. That Pia was feeling a little left out, since all the attention was on Sandhya.

"Why don't you include her in some way? Make her cut a few vegetables. Or butter the baking dish. Praise her efforts, then she won't feel excluded."

Well, Sandhya did try, but did Pia respond and do as she was told? Never. Instead, she accused Sandhya of bullying her.

"I don't have time to cut your stupid vegetables,"

she protested. "I have to go for my dance class ... after that I have computers.... and after that, my swimming lessons. I'm not your maid or assistant. Forget it... Besides, I hate your cooking. Why don't we order from Domino's?"

Sandhya had retreated, with tears stinging her eyes.

That night she logged onto Facebook and posted a status message: "Kid sisters are from hell."

Asavari who was online too, popped up to chat.

Asavari : hey, wassup? pia d pest up 2 tricks?

Sandhya : ya. feel lk klng her. thrw her out of d window.

A : i feel ur pain.

S : sch awful thoughts abt my own sis. i fl scared... n guilty.

A : dont be hrd on urself.

S : wish she were nvr brn. jst bhaiya, me, mom n dad. blssfl. no shrng a room with dat piglet. no nasty talk...

A : my lil bro's a pain 2. u know they cant hlp it. they're stl small. n we r older so we hv to be 'mature'.

14

S   : ya. i guess reacting to dem mks it wrs. grin n bear it. ☺

A   : yup

S   : flt btr tlkng to u. gtg. nite.

A   : nite ☺

Sandhya felt a little better after talking to Asavari. She put on her favourite music, the latest album of Coldplay and thought about her friendship with 'A' as she called Asavari.

Sandhya hugged a pillow and sighed. What would she do without Asavari? The one person she could confidently confide in and trust. But even Asavari did not know her secret... the whole truth, this one time.

Chapter Two

Friendship With 'A'

They'd met at their primary school interview. Asavari had come with just her father and she was holding a large doll. Sandhya had been surprised to see a child without a mother around. She'd watched Asavari's dad sitting on the hard floor of the basketball court to tie his daughter's shoelaces when they'd got undone.

She'd turned to her own mom and commented, "Look at that girl... the one with the big doll. How funny – she's with her dad. Where's her mom? And why is she hugging that doll?"

Anu had shushed her and said, "We don't know about her life... let's not stare at her like that. Maybe her mom had to go somewhere urgently. Besides, so what if she's come with her dad – nothing all that odd about it... now... stop looking at her like that... your turn is next. Good luck. Relax. Answer clearly. I'm sure you'll do very well."

Sandhya had found Asavari right next to her during the interview. She'd noticed tears streaming down her face. The teachers were being extra nice to Asavari and wiping her face. Sandhya continued to stare, even forgetting to answer when she was asked, "What does the clock say? What time is it?"

Sandhya had also noticed an anxious face peeping into the room from a small window – Asavari's dad's. Sandhya was puzzled and dying to know what the matter was. Forgetting the rest of the interview, she'd grabbed hold of Asavari and demanded, "Why are you crying so much? Where's your mother?" And that had led to more tears.

As the teachers comforted Asavari, Sandhya, unable to figure out what had happened, had abruptly left the interview midway and rushed out to look for Anu. Just then, one of the teachers had emerged from the hall and tapped Sandhya. "It's okay, dear," she'd said, "come back and finish the rest of the interview... Asavari has stopped crying now." Sandhya had refused to go back and asked to meet her mother. "No, no, no... I don't want to join this school. It is full of cry-babies," she'd said, with tears pouring out of her own eyes.

Just then, a soft male voice had intervened and Sandhya heard the person tell the teacher, "Let me handle this myself... please... leave us alone for a minute."

Sandhya had whirled around to find Asavari's dad looking at her. He'd put his arms on Sandhya's narrow shoulders, and said in a soft, gentle voice, "I understand your reaction... it's natural...but please don't get upset by my daughter's tears...you see, she doesn't have a mother... she died four months ago... Asavari... that's her name... is missing her mother a lot... and I'm trying my best to be both mom and dad to her, and to her little brother. So, I know you're a sweet girl, and you will help my daughter by not laughing at her or reacting to her crying... please... tell me your name... and please, please... help me... I need your help to see Asavari through this interview... all you have to do is smile at her... that's all... will you do that for me?"

Sandhya had felt stunned by the revelation. And also, upset with herself for being so insensitive... so mean... so cruel.

Poor thing, imagine! No mother!! Sandhya shook her head. She refused to imagine such a possibility.

What would she do without Ma? It was too awful a thought. She went back into the cheerful hall and sat on a low yellow chair. Asavari was still sobbing as Sandhya shyly reached over and held her hand.

"Don't cry," she said, "if you cry, so will I and then we will have to do this interview all over again."

Asavari stopped crying and smiled through her tears. They both looked up and stared at a large poster of Humpty Dumpty. Sandhya started lisping the poem, deliberately mispronouncing words. Asavari joined her and soon they were laughing together, much to the delight of the teachers.

"Do you know your telephone number?"

"Yeth, yeth, we do."

"Do you know your addresses?"

"Yeth, we live close by…"

"How many colours in the rainbow?"

"Vibgyor…we know…"

And that is how it went for the next ten minutes, till the interview was over and they came out of the hall skipping happily.

Would they remain "best friends for life"? Sandhya had wondered...

Chapter Three

Name, Name, Go Away

After that early encounter Sandhya and Asavari had become inseparable. They grew up spending all their free time together, shared the contents of their snack boxes (Asavari's yummy sandwiches, Sandhya's Gauritai specials) and more importantly, shared secrets. One of the first secrets involved Sandhya's feelings about her name. She recalled saying to Asavari, as they sat together in one corner of the basketball court.

"How lucky you are that your parents gave you such a cool name. Just look at mine – it's so dumb. I hate it. What sort of a name is Sandhya? Ugh. When I grow up, I'm going to change it – I've already spoken to Mom about it."

Asavari nodded sympathetically. "Yeah... it's really a dumb name. I feel bad for you. What were they thinking? My mom chose my name and it used to be Anoushka. She said it sounded Russian and she wanted me to become a ballerina; later it got changed to Asavari but I don't mind that either."

Sandhya's eyes widened. "Lucky you! Wonder what my mom thought. Maybe it was my grandmom's idea. You know my father's mother. Dadi is like a witch. She never smiles, only scolds. No matter what I do, my dadi gets furious. She seems to hate me...maybe because I'm a girl. I once heard her telling my dad, 'You have two daughters and only one son...' as if it's his fault, or Ma's fault.

"Then she glared at me and said, 'Go and study... and stop wearing all these short, tight clothes. In our time, we didn't allow our daughters to leave the house half-dressed like this. Really Beta...you must tell Bahu to keep a stricter eye on these two.'"

"I went behind her chair and made a face. Dad saw me... but didn't say anything. I think he wanted to laugh, but obviously couldn't. Even he is scared of Dadi. We call her Hitler *Memsahib*. But Dadaji is sweet. Maybe that's because he's deaf... not totally. But he only hears what he wants to. Oh yes... they both hate Zorro. And Zorro hates them. He doesn't stop barking when they visit. One day, he nearly bit Dadi when she tried to shoo him away with her *chappal*. She's old... really, really old. She likes all old things. I'm very scared of her."

The two of them ate their snacks thoughtfully, thinking about their names. Sandhya added ruefully, "My dad said I should be proud to be named after his own grandmother who was called 'Sandhya'. Big deal. I would rather be named after... after... a pop star. I don't mind being called Britney or Christina. I don't even mind being named after a tennis star. Do you play tennis? Doesn't Anna sound good? Or Maria! Or Serena?"

Asavari snapped her fingers and announced brightly, "Idea! I'll call you Anna from today. Anna, Anna, Anna, it sounds nice. It suits you. You look more like an 'Anna' with your long braids, than like some Indian goddess."

Sandhya kept quiet and finally said, "But Mom will get very angry. As for that stupid Pia, she'll tell the whole world and everybody will laugh at me."

Asavari put her arm around her friend, saying, "Don't worry, Anna! It's our secret. We won't tell anyone. It will be my special name for you. Pia will never find out."

Sandhya shook her head. "That Pia... oof... she's such a pest. I really hate her. She spies on me all the time. And then does *chugli* to Bhaiya or Mom. She'll find out my new name somehow. Then, *khatam*, even that secret will be out."

"Don't worry, Anna," Asavari said reassuringly, "next time I meet Pia, I'll give her one tight one – I'm quite good at that."

Sandhya's eyes widened, "Don't be silly. If Mom finds out my friends are slapping Pia, she'll come and complain to Miss Choksi. And then I'll get into trouble."

Asavari pulled up the sleeve of her blouse and flexed her arm.

"See," she urged Sandhya, "just see my muscles. Feel... biceps! I got them by cycling and swimming regularly. I'm so tough, even the boys in my building are scared of me. One punch and they go running, crying, 'Mummy, Mummy.' Stupid cry-babies. Don't worry Anna, I won't hit Pia, I'll only scare her by showing her my muscles."

"Anna" grinned wickedly...

If only someone would punch that pesky Pia...

Chapter Four

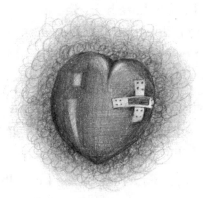

Grief Divided

The time came sooner than the two girls expected. One day Asavari came over to spend the afternoon at Sandhya's home. While they were listening to music and downloading some songs, Pia walked in with two of her own friends.

"Stop that rubbish," she said to Sandhya, "we want to study. I have a test tomorrow."

Sandhya said, "Well, we don't have tests till next week. And I want to listen to music. Get lost. Go somewhere else."

Pia and her friends kept standing next to the computer. "If you don't stop right now, I'll phone up

Dad in his office and tell him I'm going to fail in my term exams because you keep playing loud music and don't allow me to study."

Sandhya picked up the cordless phone and gave it to Pia. "Go ahead... I dare you... call Dad and see what he says. He'll never believe you. Call Mom also if you like. And Bhaiya... why not phone him, too?"

Pia pulled a face, while her friends giggled.

That annoyed Sandhya even more. "Get out of our space – right now – or else, you see what I do to you," she threatened.

Pia taunted, "What will you do to me, Didi? Come on, show us... do it."

That's when Asavari intervened. She got up slowly from a low chair and come close to Pia. "I'll show you what I can do," she said, flexing her muscles. "I'm tough. I've learned karate. I can beat all the boys in the neighbourhood... shall I show you what I can do?"

Pia and her friends fell silent and looked at each other. Pia turned around and said to them, "Forget it... let's go and play downstairs. Who wants to hang around here, anyway? *Chalo*. Where's the ball? We'll go to the *maidan* close by."

Asavari looked across at Sandhya and grinned.

"See... wasn't that easy? Don't take any nonsense from Pia. She's a real bully. You should deal with her like I deal with my *chutku* Duggu. He's such a pain. And now that there's no mom at home, he tries to sit on my head. But I don't let him, even if he complains constantly to Dad. He's such a little cry-baby. I call him a sissy – and he cries even more. Stupid! Anyway... I guess he misses Ma a lot."

Asavari trailed off, unable to carry on.

Sandhya held out a plate and said, "Here... have some apples... and grapes... Gauritai is so lazy; she can't get up on time and make a proper snack ever... only fruits. If I shout at her, she says, 'Tell *Memsahib*. Your mother has told me not to give you anything but fruits. Maybe she thinks you and your sister are *bakris* – ha, ha, ha.' "

Asavari tried to smile, though the tears that had welled up in her eyes, were now flowing down her cheeks.

"You are so lucky, Anna," she said, clutching Sandhya's hand. "You have a mother, and she loves you so-o-o-o much. My ma used to love me, too. She had such soft hands. And I loved her smell! She used to wear a certain perfume after her bath, and when I went into her room, she would spray a little on me too! I really miss my ma, Anna. I wish God had also taken me away with her. What is the point of living?"

Sandhya munched on a slice of apple using the 'chewing time' to think of an appropriate response. She allowed Asavari to cry in peace, sliding across a box of tissues for her friend to blow her nose. She sensed Asavari wanted to talk about her mom… maybe she hadn't really done that with anyone since the tragedy. After all, what could she have said to her dad, who must have been so sad himself? Her kid brother had been too young to understand death or remember her. Sandhya waited for Asavari to continue.

"My mom… she was the most beautiful woman in the world. Do you know, she used to model when she was young? Really!! That's how she met my dad… he was an advertising executive. He used to create ads for washing powders and other products. He chose my mom's picture for a campaign, and they fell in love. She had lovely eyes, brown and soft. I wish God had given me her eyes… so sad na? My dad says I look like her, but I don't think so… see my potato nose? Hers was straight. See my hair? Her hair was silky. Dad is just saying all this to make me feel better. But nothing can. Nobody can be like my mom. Sometimes she'd get so angry with me, but even when she shouted and made me cry, I still loved her. Now I feel bad that I used to trouble her… maybe I was jealous… just a little. And I would do crazy things to attract her attention. Dad tells me not to think of those times, but remember Mom smiling and laughing always."

Asavari trailed off… She seemed lost in her own world, buried in very private memories. Suddenly, she came out of her trance and announced, "I want to die… I want to be with Mom."

Sandhya shot to her feet and hugged Asavari, who had started to weep, her body shaking, her hands trembling.

What could Sandhya possibly do to comfort her best friend now??

Chapter Five

A Secret Shared

When Sandhya finally spoke, she did so gently, softly. She held Asavari's hand and said, "Don't say that... your dad needs you. So does your brother, even if he's a pain. Your mom would have wanted you to stay strong for the family. And... and... I'm there... my parents are there... especially my mom. She always asks about you."

Just as Sandhya uttered those words, in walked Anuradha, smiling brightly, and holding a large package in her hands. "Surprise, girls! Pizza. I finished work early. And I'm in a good mood. So I thought why not treat the kids to something really, really unhealthy and awful? Good idea?"

Both girls jumped up at the sight of the pizza.

"Where's Pia?"

Sandhya made a face, but her mother was quick to interrupt. "Don't tell me you've fought again... oh dear... tell me Asavari... do you fight with your brother like this?"

Asavari looked uncertainly at Sandhya, wondering what to say. Sandhya exclaimed, "Mom!! Please... you are embarrassing Asavari."

Anu was surprised. She put the pizza carton down and held up her hands.

"Sorry," she said with a laugh. "But these two fight like wildcats all the time... and I was wondering how other children behave."

Asavari said hesitantly, "Aunty... even I hate my brother Aryan... he's such a *chuglimaster* and cry-baby. The problem is, my dad always takes his side and scolds me, even when it isn't my fault at all."

Anu went over to Asavari and put her arms around her shoulders. "It's not like that, darling. Maybe your father feels a little protective towards your brother – he's younger, isn't he? Parents don't take sides. Your dad loves both of you equally. I'm sure you know that in your heart of hearts..."

Asavari nodded. "I guess so... but it's still such a problem. Aryan is so mean – he spoils all my things. He's broken my music system. He doesn't know how to behave with our dog. He's just so horrible. But Dad doesn't ever punish him – ever! Especially after my ma... after she... after her..." Anu hugged Asavari close and rocked her gently.

Anu realised the little girl was deeply upset and didn't want anyone to see her tears. Anu signalled to Sandhya with her eyes to play some music and then, in silence, the three of them just sat very still on a comfortable sofa, listening to the strains of Pandit Shivkumar Sharma's soothing santoor. The sun was setting and the room was bathed in a warm orange glow. Sandhya looked at her mother's serene expression and reminded herself of how lucky she was to have her. Asavari had stopped crying and was listening intently to the music.

"What instrument is he playing? Is it a sitar?" she asked Anu.

"No, darling, this is known as the santoor – it is played with two delicate tongs. The santoor is a stringed instrument like the sitar, but it is placed in front of the seated musician. The sounds it produces are lilting – like gently gurgling brooks over smooth stone pebbles. Don't you love this *raag*? It is called Poorvi, and is an evening *raag*. Panditji is one of India's finest musicians. Next time there's a concert in Mumbai, I'll definitely take Sandhya and you."

Asavari nodded. Sandhya spoke up after a pause, "But Mom... what about the Bryan Adams concert? You'd promised you'd get tickets. I also reminded Dad."

Anu smiled. "Catch you missing that! I haven't forgotten. But the booking starts next week. Asavari darling, why don't you join us? Shall I get permission from your dad?"

Asavari's eyes lit up. "Yes, please! That would be super. Oh... but Dad's in Delhi today. He'll be back late at night."

Anu smiled at the excitement the news had unleashed. "Girls! Girls! Calm down... and attack the pizza while it's still hot."

Asavari and Sandhya tore the carton open and greedily pounced on the piping hot pizza.

"Leave a piece for Pia," Anu instructed.

"Never!" Sandhya shouted back. "Let her starve."

Anu shook her head, muttering, "These girls are

impossible. When will they stop squabbling?"

Sandhya repeated, "Never, never, never!" with glee, as she stuffed a slice of pepperoni pizza into her mouth and watched in amazement as Asavari managed to gobble an entire portion in one big bite.

Anu's parting words were, "Don't behave like such *junglees*, you two. You are young ladies now – let's see some good manners."

The two girls exchanged looks.

"Mother talk," whispered Sandhya, and then bit her tongue. Ouch. How insensitive to say that, she said to herself, remembering with a sudden lurch of her heart that a reference like that would definitely remind Asavari of her own mom.

Thankfully for Sandhya, Asavari grinned and said, "Well – I don't have to hear it any more, do I?"

That made Sandhya feel worse. She reached out for Asavari's hand and found that she'd clenched her fingers into a tight fist. Sandhya loosened them up one by one.

"Why do you do that? Habit?" she asked.

"No... not a habit. I started after Mom was gone... each time I think of her, I clench my fist, to stop the tears. It works – really. But because I think of her so often, my fingers get a little stiff from all that clenching! You are so lucky, Sandhya, your mother loves you so much."

And they both fell silent thinking of their mothers.

Just then Bhaiya burst into the room. "Hello grannies! My God! What are you two up to sitting so quietly, with your hands in your laps? Tell me, Sandhya, have you upset Pia again? I found her complaining to someone over the phone. Perhaps she was talking to Dad. In which case, you've really had it. Good luck!"

Sandhya looked all innocence as she said, "Bhaiya... why does everybody blame me? As if she's some angel and can't do anything wrong. Ask Asavari... ask Gauritai... ask Mom... I didn't do a thing... she's just a stupid cry-baby."

Bhaiya put down his sports gear and pulled off his thick sports socks.

"Torn. Everything gets torn in this house. I don't have a single pair of good socks left. Are you sure you haven't been 'borrowing' them?"

Sandhya looked at her brother and snapped, "Why

should I bother to borrow your smelly, torn socks? I have my own. In fact, Dad was saying he can't find his socks these days... you'd better have a good answer ready for him."

As they were arguing, Anu walked in to check what was going on. "Straight into the shower, young man... off you go. And by the way, have you taken Dad's favourite after-shave? He's been looking for it."

Sandhya stuck out her tongue at Sid and said, "There! I told you so... bet you've been *maro-ing* other things, too. I heard him shouting at Gauritai last week. His badminton tracks were missing."

Sid threw his dirty socks rolled up into a ball, straight at Sandhya. "Stay out of it, okay? Mind your own business. Or else, I'll tell Mom about... about... forget it. You can tell her yourself if you have the guts."

Anu raised her eyebrow and asked Sandhya, "Something important I need to know? What is it? Come on darling, out with it."

Sandhya looked stricken. "It's... it's nothing Mama... really... Bhaiya is just acting smart... chill." But Anu knew her daughter too well.

She left the room saying, "I'm in no hurry... I'm sure

you'll tell me whatever it is, when you're ready. By the way... What did you do to Pia? Why is she crying?"

Sandhya rolled her eyes skywards. "I have done nothing to her... absolutely nothing. But now I will... grrrrr... I hate her. Why don't you give her away to someone? But who will have such a kid?"

Anu shook her head reproachfully. "Don't keep saying that. You may think it's a big joke. But it really affects Pia."

Sandhya shot back. "It is not at all a joke. I mean it... please Mom... it's impossible to live with her day in and day out. I think you should look for a good boarding school."

Anu looked over her shoulder and asked, "For whom? You or her?"

Sandhya hit her forehead with the flat of her hand and said exasperatedly, "Her, of course. Why me? She's a pig and a pest. Look at how much she eats all day. And then leaves sticky wrappers all over our room. And on my side of the bed. She's the dirtiest, most horrible girl I know. Asavari is so lucky. She only has a younger brother. And he's so sweet."

Asavari shook her head vehemently. "No, he isn't. He's horrid, too. Do you know what he did yesterday? He rubbed chocolate ice cream all over the wall. And then tried to lick it off! Eeeks!! Good thing my dad wasn't home."

"Well," said Anu, "it's nearly time for Sandhya's father to be here... thanks for reminding me, Asavari. I'd better organise a snack for him. I hope Bhaiya hasn't sent Gauritai out on some errand of his."

Pia ran in, screaming, "I told Dad! I told Dad! Now wait and see what he does to you... and if you act mean again, I'll tell Mom everything."

Sandhya picked up the nearest object (mercifully, it wasn't either hard or heavy) and threw it at her sister.

Pia ducked just in time and yelled, "Bhaiya, come here fast... Didi is trying to kill me."

Sandhya was really, really mad by then and had started to fling any and every object that wasn't nailed down. It was beginning to look like a full-scale missile war.

Sid came up behind Sandhya and pinned her arms to her sides. "Stop it... Will you? This is disgusting. I'm going to speak to both Mom and Dad about you two girls. I can't believe you were going to chuck all these things at Pia! Mom's favourite crystal bowl! Are you nuts?"

Asavari placed a restraining hand on Sandhya's

arm. "Chill, *yaar*," she said, "it's okay. Drop it."

Sandhya took a few deep breaths and put down her mother's precious bowl. "One of these days...," she muttered under her breath, "... really... one of these days that devil is really going to get it from me."

Asavari picked up her things to leave. "Must go," she said hurriedly.

"Wait," said Sandhya, "take this with you..." and she thrust a CD into her friend's hand. "You'll love it... great mix... I've burnt it myself... Beyonce, Madonna, Punjabi rap, Strings, Shubha Mudgal... Adnan Sami, Rabbi, Norah Jones... Amjad Ali... Rihanna."

"Wow!" said Asavari gratefully. "Cool... I'll hear it in the car."

Anu came out of the kitchen and said, "Just a minute, darling... here... take a few homemade *chaklis* and *chivda* and some brownies... share them with your baby brother and dad."

Asavari said, "Thank you so much, Aunty. You're always so sweet... my dad always says I'm lucky to know you."

"Oh... it's nothing," Anu said, "... these girls are always nagging me about making snacks at home. Today, I had a little time, so I decided to make a small batch... it's from a ready mix, okay? Easy. No talent required!"

Everybody laughed as Sandhya escorted Asavari to the door, whispering, "Don't tell anybody what I told you... nobody, promise? If Mom finds out from someone else, I'll be in even deeper trouble."

Asavari placed a finger on her lips and said, "Sssh... don't worry. I won't even tell Dad, though I don't keep a single secret from him, just as Mom had made me promise. She'd said, 'Remember, now you only have Dad to lean on. Tell him everything just as you used to tell me. He needs to know, or else, how can he help you?' When Dad and I go for a walk around the Race Course every evening, he asks me what happened during the day, and I tell him... better that way, na?"

Sandhya nodded her head in agreement."Yes... much better... but this secret is between us... okay?"

Asavari hugged Sandhya and said, "Don't worry... it will be okay. Your mom is so sweet, she'll understand."

Before going to bed that night Sandhya wondered if Mom would really understand if she knew what she was hiding...

Chapter Six

Bhoot! Bhoot!

Sandhya worried about this for some time and then dropped off to sleep. She was rudely awakened by Pia in the middle of the night.

"Didi... I saw someone... something... swear. Must be a *bhoot*. Look... look... right there. And I heard a tapping noise as well."

Sandhya reached for her bedside clock and checked the time. "Pia! It's 3 a.m.! Just go back to sleep, okay? I have to get up early tomorrow for marching practice. Our House is going to win this year. Here... drink some water. SLEEP!!"

But Pia refused to either switch off the light or stop

talking. "Don't believe me if you don't want to... let the *bhoot* come and sit on your neck and strangle you. Gauritai said there are male *bhoots* and female *bhoots*. It is the girl *bhoots* who are the worst. This one must be a girl."

Sandhya put a pillow over her head and turned to one side. "Keep talking... I'm not listening. I can't hear... girl *bhoot*, boy *bhoot*... that Gauritai is mad and you don't have to listen to all her rubbish."

Pia kept quiet for a few seconds before prodding Sandhya again. "See... did you see that? Just outside our window, behind the curtain. It's a large *bhoot* and a very angry *bhoot*. Just hear the noise it's making."

"Shut up Pia... I told you, I have to wake up early."

"But Didi... I'm very scared. What if the *bhoot* crashes through the window and eats me up?"

Pia continued whining. Sandhya reached over and pinched Pia. "There... that's the *bhoot*.And if you don't shut up, the *bhoot* will pinch you even harder, got it?"

Pia began to cry. "You are always so mean to me. No other Didi behaves this way. I asked all my friends. I asked Payal and Fatima. I asked Rohita and Binaisha

... all of them have older sisters – nobody like you. I hope that *bhoot* takes you away."

Sandhya got out of bed and switched on all the lights. "Okay. Where's the *bhoot*... show me. And if you can't produce the *bhoot*, I will take all your pillows and throw them on the floor."

Pia pointed to the window. "Look there... the *bhoot* is dancing now," she said, her voice quaking with fear.

"Dancing? Maybe it's Michael Jackson's *bhoot*, in that case... come on, let's put on *Beat It*, and join the dance. Maybe we can teach the *bhoot* a few new steps. Maybe the *bhoot* wants to take lessons in moon-walking."

Pia scowled, "If you make fun of me, I'll wake up Mom and Dad. Then see what happens. I'll scream so loudly, even Bhaiya will get up. Then he'll come and show you properly."

"Call him, call him," Sandhya challenged. "If he does anything to me, I'll tell Dad who broke his cologne bottle, who stained his T-shirt, who punched extra holes in his belt."

Pia suddenly screamed and clutched Sandhya's arm. "Didi... the *bhoot* is waving...please Didi... please...do something."

Sandhya turned towards the window reluctantly and saw a large shadow. For a brief moment, the sight of the shadow unnerved her as well. Then she took a few long strides to the large window and threw it open. Pia shut her eyes tightly and screamed.

"Silly girl," Sandhya scolded, "open your eyes and see what your *bhoot* is... go on... open them."

Gingerly, Pia opened first one eye and then the other. "Didi... I'm sorry I woke you up... Didi... don't tell Mom, okay. Didi... I promise I'll never do this again... but Didi... it did look like a ghost... admit it... even you got scared."

Sandhya smiled and tousled Pia's hair. "Silly girl. Both of us forgot the building is being painted. The scaffolding is still there, and the painters have left the gunny sacks hanging from the bamboos. Because it's so windy tonight, some of the gunny sacks have come loose and are flapping in the breeze – that's all. Come on... let's sleep, before someone sees the light on in our room. Bhaiya will never wake up – he sleeps like Kumbhakaran. But Mom is such a light sleeper... ssh... go to bed. We'll tell her everything in the morning."

Sandhya lay awake for a long time, staring at the ceiling of the room she shared with Pia. She could hear the soft, musical tinkle of the wind chime their mother had hung over the window sill. Sandhya quite liked her room, even though she complained a lot about certain things, like not having an air-conditioner, when Bhaiya had one in his room. Dad had promised the room would have one soon. But when? It was so hot during summer. And the monsoon was even worse, since she couldn't keep the windows open. It wasn't fair.

But Dad always lectured them. "When your mother and I were students, we never had all these fancy facilities, we studied under a ceiling fan and never felt the heat. You children are getting a bit too spoilt."

Sandhya sighed. All her friends had air-conditioners. Asavari's room was amazing – with everything that matched so well – the curtains, furniture, bedspread. Her own room looked… not that bad… not as bad as Swati's but still. She wanted a new computer. And her cupboard was broken at the hinges.

The colour scheme was so babyish. Mom had thought of it when she and Pia were little kids. But now they were not that little!! She didn't like pink and nearly everything in the room was icky-pink, including the paint on the dressing table. Sandhya wanted an up-to-date room, like the ones she saw in teen movies on TV. What fabulous fittings those rooms had, with great gadgets, plasma screens, wall units, even mini-fridges! Each time she asked Mom and Dad, they said next year... next year...Sheeesh! When would that year come? When she was thirty? Anyway... that was that. But at least Mom had agreed to change the curtains soon. And the bathroom mirror which was broken, was also getting replaced. Parents always said, "Patience!" But that wasn't fair on kids, was it?

The girls overslept and missed all the early-morning commotion.

Chapter Seven

It's An Emergency!

When the girls entered the kitchen rubbing their eyes sleepily, they found Gauritai making *dosas* for their breakfast.

"Where's Mom?" Sandhya asked Gauritai.

"How come she left without saying bye to us?" Pia asked as Gauritai continued to flip the *dosa* into a crisp, neat roll.

"Don't ask me!" she replied. "I heard the phone ringing while it was still dark outside. When the milk arrived, I noticed a light in the passage. I thought Bhaiya had arrived late last night and forgotten to switch it off. Then, I saw *Memsahib's* sandals were

46

missing from their usual place. And she didn't ask for tea at 6.30 as she normally does. When I went to *Sahib's* table with his *nashta* at 7, he said your mother had to go somewhere in a hurry. He mentioned it was something serious and urgent. After that I got busy myself."

The two girls looked at each other.

"What about Bhaiya?" Sandhya enquired.

Gauritai sighed. "You know your bhaiya – he can sleep through an earthquake. Check his room – he must be there."

Sandhya wondered aloud, "Maybe Dad's having a shower. I'll go check."

And she left, with Pia shouting, "But Didi – what about your marching practice? You'll get late... then your House will get minus points."

Sandhya wasn't listening as she knocked on the door of her parents' room. No answer. That was strange. Dad always called out from the shower when he heard a knock. And what was more, the TV was off! Dad never missed the breakfast news. Sandhya went straight into the room without waiting for a response. The room was empty and stranger still, it was untidy. Both her parents were finicky, fastidious people who never left towels or discarded clothes lying around the room... and the sight that greeted Sandhya was as if a tornado had hit the place. Dad and Mom had obviously left in a great hurry.

She immediately rushed to the cordless phone on Dad's bedside table and called her mother's mobile – no response. Ditto for Dad's. By now Pia had walked into the room and was looking really, really worried.

"Let's wake up Bhaiya, come on... I don't care if he shouts, screams and throws something at us... We have to tell him, okay?"

They banged on Sid's door expecting to hear a stream of "get lost... go away... stop that noise."

Instead Sid quietly opened the door and to their amazement, he was fully dressed.

"Bhaiya!" Sandhya exclaimed. "Something's happened... Mom and Dad are missing."

Sid said in a quiet, calm voice, "They've gone to the hospital... Nana has had a heart attack... but... don't worry... he's going to be okay. I'm going there right now myself. You girls behave yourselves... I've told Gauritai to keep an eye on you when you get back from school. Mom will call as soon as she can. And

I guess you'll catch Dad in the office after a couple of hours."

Pia broke the silence that followed by asking, "Is he going to die? Don't people die after a heart attack? My friend Reenu's dad died of a heart attack – and he was so young. Nana is ancient! I'm sure he'll pop it..."

Sandhya glared angrily at her sister. "Just shut up. You are so dumb. Don't say such things. Bhaiya said he's going to be fine. We don't want to know about other people who're dead... you always talk utter rubbish."

Pia looked sullenly at Sandhya and stuck out her tongue. "I knew someone was going to die when I saw that *bhoot*... Must've been Nana's *bhoot*... take a bet."

Sid caught his kid sister by her shoulders and spoke in his sternest voice. "I never want to hear you say such insensitive things – got it? All those silly friends of yours... don't think I can't hear your phone conversations. Now, just keep quiet or else I'll rap you. "

Pia squared her shoulders and said, "Try rapping me. *I'll tell Mom.*"

Sid moved towards her menacingly. "Yeah? You'll tell Mom, huh? Well, by then, I'd have broken your jaw ... let me see what you tell her when you won't be able to speak... now buzz off."

Sandhya took Sid aside and asked worriedly, "Nana will be fine – right? God ... I hope nothing happens to him... Oh God... I've kept my fingers tightly crossed. Mom must be so worried... Thank God she's a doc... now all her doc friends will help her."

Sid nodded and said, "Don't know when we'll be back. You make sure that brat behaves herself. Don't let her talk non-stop on the phone – we should keep the lines free, in case... well... in case of anything. Okay? See you later."

With that Sid was gone, leaving Sandhya to think about her grandfather.

Get well soon, she said silently. She felt sad that she hadn't been able to spend much time with him and Nani. She remembered the time when she was much younger and all of them would go off to Matheran for the summer. Nana and Nani would actually jog with the family in the morning, go for a swim, even accompany the kids on horseback at sunset. Nana was such fun to be with – full of stories of his days as an adventurous tea planter. Sometimes, he used to exaggerate wildly and tell the family all sorts of tall stories. But Sandhya would hang on to every word and say, "Please Nana, tell us that one about the tiger once again... or the other one about the time a herd of wild elephants charged your jeep, and how you shooed them away... and the other story about a leopard, who strayed into your garden looking for chickens..." while the others rolled their eyes skyward and groaned, "Oh no... not those stories again."

Nana would gently lead Sandhya to a swing in the garden and begin yet another version of the familiar tale. During the narration, he'd point to various birds flitting from one mango tree to the next, and divert Sandhya's attention with a sub-plot about parrots, sparrows, crows and mynahs. She couldn't believe the same man – so tall, so strong – could now be lying on a hospital bed, fighting for his life. Sandhya decided to make him a cheerful get-well-soon card.

It was a tradition in their family. They always made cards for one another. It was Nani who'd started the practice. She'd once said, "It's so easy to ask your parents for twenty rupees and buy a card. Why not create your own card? People who receive it feel special... besides, it's more personal and creative."

Sandhya remembered protesting at the time, "But Nani, my handwriting is terrible... and I can't draw... see my art book... it's so messy."

But Nani had sat her down and said, "Go and fetch some old magazines, get a few crayons, dried leaves, sequins, coloured threads and we'll make something together."

Sandhya had watched in fascination as Nani used simple materials to cut colourful shapes which she stuck on card paper. "Now... you write your own message. Try composing a poem, or if that's difficult, create a little story about the person and the occasion. I've left lots of space inside."

Sandhya had struggled for half-an-hour. And then, somehow, the words had presented themselves to her.

After that first personalised card, Sandhya had never had to spend her meagre pocket money buying one. Now, so many years later, Sandhya's cards were famous even in school. Teachers looked forward to receiving them on Teachers' Day. And all her friends told her they'd preserved the cards because each one was so unique!

Even Zorro had sensed something was wrong in the house. He hadn't touched his breakfast. For Zorro to give up his milk and biscuits meant he was really, really upset. Gauritai tried hard to coax him, using the same baby talk that she used with Sandhya and

Pia when they refused to eat *khichdi* and *dahi* during fevers. But Zorro turned away, preferring to mope in his favourite spot, right next to the refrigerator. Sandhya knew he was enjoying the brief blast of cold air each time the fridge door opened.

Gauritai shook her head and said, "It's been ten hours but Zorro hasn't touched food or water. Even these dumb creatures know when someone is sick – that is God's miracle."

Pia butted in, "Or maybe Zorro is also sick of your food, the way I am."

Sandhya snapped, "How dare you say that to Gauritai? Say sorry at once."

Pia stamped her foot and said, "Why should I say sorry? Look at what other girls bring in their snack boxes and look at the yucky stuff we eat. I also want cool snacks... grilled sandwiches, pasta, pizza. I feel so bad to find only dumb fruits or *chappati-bhaji*."

Sandhya said sharply, "It's not Gauritai's fault. That's what Ma wants us to eat. She knows what's good for us. She's a doctor."

Pia burst out angrily, "Well, sometimes I wish she was a nobody and not a fancy doctor. Just a mom, like all those other moms. Instead of saving other people's kids, she should look after her own properly. Whenever I tell her to take me shopping, she says, 'Not today… I have an emergency operation.' Ha! What about our 'emergencies' huh?"

Sandhya lunged at her sister. It was Zorro who saved Pia, by jumping in between the warring sisters in the nick of time.

Sandhya decided to draw a tea garden for her grandpa. She knew he loved his days in Munnar and often talked about retiring there. But where would she find appropriate pictures? She rushed to the computer to see what she could find on the Internet. Sure enough, she found Munnar in no time. The website itself was so beautiful, she got lost navigating all the links.

The phone rang and broke the spell. Sandhya grabbed the receiver and asked, "How is he?"

There was a slight tremor in Anu's voice as she tried to control her emotions while reassuring her daughter. "We don't know yet… he's in the Intensive Care Unit, darling. The specialists are not saying anything at this stage. Just pray for him."

Sandhya was still and silent, as she continued to listen numbly to her mother's various instructions.

Finally, she asked, "And Nani? How is she?"

Anu answered, "Calm and strong. You know your nani... she's one person who never gives up. She's really amazing."

Sandhya smiled and let out a long breath. "Thank God, Mom... now I know Nana will be just fine."

The whole family (except Pia who was too young) helped keep Nana company at the hospital. Dad used to go directly from the office, while Ma frequently stayed the night, allowing Nani to go home herself and get some rest. Sandhya hated hospital smells and sights. But she forced herself to visit her grandfather every other day. Bhaiya and she would make a plan, and often Asavari too, came with them.

One day Sandhya ran straight into Akshi in the hospital corridor. He was the handsome cricket captain of the boy's school nearby. Every girl had a massive crush on him.

"Hi," Akshi smiled, "aren't you at St. Anne's?"

Sandhya nodded dumbly.

Akshi held out his right hand saying, "I'm Akshay, St. Peter's next door to your school."

Shaking his hand limply, Sandhya stuttered, "I'm S...S... Sandy."

Introducing herself as Sandhya was unthinkable!

Sandhya asked in a calm voice that belied her jelly-like insides, "So what are you doing here?"

He smiled, "Same thing as you are I suppose – visiting a sick relative?"

"My nanaji," Sandhya mumbled, flushed with embarrassment, her hand going straight to her hair. Oh God! She had to be wearing that bright pink scrunchy on her ponytail just today!!

"Your hair looks really good when you don't tie it up," Akshi commented.

"Really?" Sandhya asked with an incredulous note in her voice.

"Yes, really," Akshi answered.

"Oh… cool. Er... I thought you played really well in the inter-school cricket match last week," Sandhya stuttered.

"Okay… not bad…84 runs. Next time, I'll aim for a century," Akshi grinned.

Suddenly, glancing at his watch, he exclaimed, "Oh, I'd better be going! My masi's waiting for this soup I'm carrying. Listen, why don't we exchange cell numbers? It might be useful considering both our folks are admitted to the same hospital."

Sandhya nodded, struggling hard to contain her excitement.

Then, cell numbers exchanged, they stood in the corridor in silence for a few seconds.

"Okay, see you," Sandhya trailed off uncertainly.

"Sure... and... your hair... no ponytail," Akshi teased before walking away! Sandhya was too excited to even wish Nani and Nana when she entered the room. Instead, she rushed to the bathroom to stare at herself.

Her long nutmeg-coloured hair framed her oval face, and her large, dark eyes with thick lashes resembled deep pools. Sandhya pulled a face. She didn't like her teeth ("too prominent"), and she hated her eyebrows ("too thick"). But her mouth was well shaped – not too pouty, not too thin-lipped. And her ears were perfect. She stood on her toes to see more of herself. Not too tall (5'4"), not too fat (waist size 26"), she concluded she was just about okay. But her classmate Mansi was prettier. So was Naima. Sandhya sighed. Akshi would probably forget all about the hospital meeting. But she would remember it forever!

She was still grinning goofily when she reached home. The beeping of her phone startled her. It was an SMS, from Akshi! Sandhya's hands trembled as she pressed the buttons. The text popped up : Nice bmpng into u 2 day. Hp ur nanaji gts wl soon. C u smtm sandy 😊

Sandhya felt her knees go weak. Her head was in the clouds when she walked into the study. Her reverie was rudely shattered when she saw Pia in the room. She had jammed a CD in the player yet again!

Chapter Eight

Big Fight Over Small Screen

The pest was also refusing to get off Sandhya's favourite chair. What was worse, Pia had hidden the remote control panel, so all Sandhya could do was fume.

"I have told Mom a million times – pleeeease get me my own TV... even a *chhota* one. And pleeeeease get me my own music system – I don't care if it's the cheapest in the market. I hate sharing with you. I hate listening to your weird tracks and watching those dumb serials."

Pia looked up with a cheeky smile and retorted, "Oh yeah?" But she didn't move.

Sandhya hung around for a few seconds and then stomped out.

Within minutes, she was back again yelling, "Pia... you donkey... did you borrow my blue T-shirt again? And I can't find my shorts... My jeans are missing as well."

Pia lazily replied, "Why shout at me? Ask Gauritai. She must've lost them as usual. Or maybe they're still in the laundry."

Sandhya walked up to her kid sister and shook her hard. "Don't you dare give me attitude. Just tell where my things are ... or ... or ... I'll bash you up. And give me the remote. Haaaw! What are you watching? You know you're not supposed to see *Friends*! Even I'm not allowed... you... you... just wait... watching all these adult serials at your age, aren't you ashamed?"

Pia laughed – a ha-ha-ha laugh. "If Mom and Dad don't let me watch it at our home, I'll go to Jai's or Deepa's... I'll go anywhere. Everybody in my class watches *Friends*. It's so cool."

Sandhya snapped, "I don't care what *everybody* does in your class – this serial is not meant for your age group – that's it."

Pia mocked, "So... what should I watch instead –

Ramayana? Cartoons? *Bhajans?* Doordarshan?"

Sandhya thought for a bit and said, "Kids your age watch the Discovery Channel, National Geographic – or any of the music channels... not *Friends* with all those dialogues. Do you even understand what they're saying, huh?"

Pia stuck her fingers into her ears and screamed, "Shooooooo! Ssssh!! Go away."

As she did that, the remote control slipped out from behind her and fell on the floor. Sandhya grabbed it, switched the channel and tried to push Pia out of her favourite, comfy chair. Pia resisted and Sandhya's nail accidentally scratched Pia's cheek in the scuffle. Pia let out a blood-curdling scream which brought Gauritai rushing out of the kitchen.

"Baby!! What are you doing?" she demanded, as Pia continued to scream with her eyes screwed tight.

Sandhya, looking guilty, said, "I didn't mean it... it was an accident. Please get some ice... no, get an antiseptic cream... quickly."

By then, Pia's screams had subsided and great big tears were flowing down her face.

"She always does this to me... always. Today, she

scratched me so badly... tomorrow she could strangle me... or stab me."

Gauritai put her arms around Pia and comforted her. "You girls should stop fighting... really... I'll go crazy one day."

The doorbell rang just then. Their mom! Sandhya looked stricken while Pia pumped up the volume of her howling. Anu walked in calmly and surveyed the scene. She put her handbag down and ignored Pia's howling. Turning to Sandhya, she gestured to her to come into the room.

"What's the story this time?" she asked, keeping her voice steady. Sandhya started to explain, but her words came pouring out in a garbled, incoherent stream.

Anu closed her eyes briefly and said, "Look... I'm tired. And worried about your grandfather. I really don't need this nonsense. You are not a child anymore. I expect more responsible behaviour from you."

Sandhya felt awfully guilty. Nana had come home after twenty days in hospital. Twenty, tension-filled days when the children hardly saw their mother. She looked down and muttered, "Sorry... I'm really sorry, Ma. But that Pia..." She had to leave her sentence unfinished as Mom raised her hand.

"Enough. *Bas*. Stop it... I don't want to hear any more. Please ask Gauritai to get me a cup of tea... no sugar. I'm going to lie down for a while."

Sandhya left the room feeling sheepish and silly. She told herself she would never behave in such an irresponsible way again, no matter how hard Pia tried to provoke her.

Sandhya felt selfish about not having thought of her mother's feelings at that moment. But she also felt angry and resentful at always having to be 'responsible', 'mature', 'helpful', only because she happened to be born a few years before that brat Pia. It's not fair, she frequently argued. After all, I didn't ask to be born before her. And so what if she was younger? That shouldn't be an excuse for ever and ever!

Pia was not such a baby now – she was nine years old – old enough to control her bawling. And yet nobody said anything to her. Not Dad. Not even Bhaiya. Everybody treated her like she was two years old. Anyway – Mom's tea! Oh God!! She'd completely forgotten to instruct Gauritai!

Chapter Nine

Pia Spills The Beans

When Sandhya went in search of Gauritai, she discovered she'd gone to do the washing. Sandhya tried knocking on the door of the tiny utility room, but Gauritai shooed her away. Mom was waiting. There was just one thing to do – make the tea herself. She was a good cook. Well...her cakes were gobbled up greedily by everyone. But she didn't really know how to make Mom's tea. Mom drank her cuppa in a particular way and she was really fussy about it. Sandhya walked into the kitchen and started to look around for tea leaves, sugar, strainer and kettle. She noticed Pia watching from the doorway and decided to ignore her.

Mom would call out any moment and fire her for not telling Gauritai on time. Pia inched into the kitchen slowly, till she was right behind Sandhya. "Need help?" she asked in a small voice.

"Yeah... but not yours, thank you," Sandhya snapped.

"But... but... I know how Mom's tea is made... I watch Gauritai every day... the tea leaves are not in that cabinet, they're over there, on the other side."

Sandhya ignored Pia and started looking for the electric kettle.

"Didi... Didi... Gauritai keeps the kettle under that shelf... I'll show you."

Sandhya whirled around. "You stay out of it... I don't need your stupid help. All you do is get me into trouble with Ma... that too when it isn't my fault."

Pia pouted and parked herself on the tall stool – the one Bhaiya always sat on to wolf down snacks.

"Fine. Don't take my help then... Gauritai may take two hours inside... Maybe three, four, five... then see what Mom will say."

Sandhya had by then found all that she was looking for. She decided to arrange the tea-tray prettily, with a flourish or two. A small vase with a single rose, just as they showed in all those fancy TV commercials, and a brightly-coloured serviette would add a nice touch, she figured. As for the tea, well, Mom liked hers very hot and very light. Milk? Most times Mom had hers without.

But Sandhya decided to heat some in a pan anyway – just to make the tea-tray look good.

"Do you know how to light the gas?" Pia asked.

"Of course, I do," replied Sandhya testily. "Why... do you think I'm a complete duh? You have obviously forgotten all the cakes! You light it, if you think you are all that smart! You know I don't like to strike matches. I prefer ovens."

Pia taunted, "Well... make tea in that oven of yours then."

She watched with a sly grin as Sandhya fumbled. This was going to be great fun, Pia thought, as Sandhya couldn't strike the damp matches or locate the automatic gas lighter.

"Mom will wonder whether Gauritai has gone to milk the cow," Pia laughed.

Sandhya gave her a dirty look and continued to struggle with the matchbox.

Pia giggled. "Phone Bhaiya on his cell and ask him how he lights his cigarettes," she suggested wickedly.

Sandhya stopped what she was doing and gasped,

"What?? Bhaiya... smokes? I don't believe it. Oh God... if Mom and Dad find out, he's dead!"

Pia clapped her hands with glee. "Very good... now let Bhaiya get into trouble for a change."

Sandhya was so shocked, she forgot all about her mother's tea. "How do you know?" she started to ask Pia, before noticing Anu at the kitchen door.

Both girls fell silent and stared at each other, wondering how much their mother had heard. Anu walked in and took over the tea-making while asking casually, "Where's Gauritai. Hanging up the washing? And Sandhya what is wrong with you today.... What have you done with all these tea leaves? I only need a tablespoon for my cup!"

Sandhya stuttered, "Mom... the thing is... I wasn't sure...the matches..."

Anu smiled, "Don't worry... won't take a minute."

Within minutes, Anu had settled on a collapsible chair, and was sipping a steaming cup of tea. After a few seconds she said, "I overheard your conversation... sorry... couldn't help it! Pia... are you sure you know what you're saying about Bhaiya smoking? Because, if it isn't true, you'll be in serious trouble."

Pia was looking nervous by now. "I'm not sure... Maybe I'm wrong... I don't know... I mean, I haven't seen him smoking as such... but..."

Anu interrupted Pia. "But, what? Come on, tell me. It's okay. I won't let him know it was you who gave away his secret. It's very important for Dad and me to know this, because it concerns Bhaiya's health. He is an athlete... he needs stamina. If he smokes, how will he play any games? If he's experimenting with cigarettes, we can help him quit at this stage. If you don't tell me what you know now, you'll be harming Bhaiya in the long run."

Pia rushed to her mother and hugged her. "Please Mom, please, don't get angry with Bhaiya... I only saw him once... I'm not sure whether he even lit the cigarette – really. Maybe he was just fooling around."

Anu calmed her daughter and said gently, "I will handle it... leave it to Dad and me... remember, you are not sneaking on Bhaiya... you are doing him a big, big favour... in a way, you are saving his life. Okay?"

Pia nodded, while Sandhya helped Anu clear the tray. It was going to be a long time before Bhaiya came home. And Sandhya was really worried for him. She thought about sending a text message, warning her brother, then decided it was better to let Mom and Dad handle it their way.

She was on edge the rest of the evening waiting for Bhaiya to come home and the impending storm.

Oh God! How would Bhaiya handle the outburst?

Chapter Ten

Gauritai's Story

Bhaiya called to say he was held up at his friend's home. Sandhya took the call, while she was in the midst of completing her natural history project.

"Bhaiya... have you spoken to Mom today?" she asked hesitantly.

Sid thought for a bit and replied, "Yes... sure... a couple of times. I'd called to ask about Nana...why?"

Sandhya said, "Oh... nothing... I was wondering whether Mom asked you about... about... never mind. Let her ask when you come home."

Sid said briskly, "Look, I'm in a rush. Is it something to do with Nana? If not, I'm sure it can wait. *Chal*, see you later. In case... in case... Sonali or someone calls... take a message. Write it down properly. Bye..."

Sandhya smiled. "Bhaiya... Bhaiya...," she started to say, but Sid had already disconnected.

"He's really going to have it today," she thought worriedly. "First the cigarettes, now his girlfriend... Mom will really lose it... poor Bhaiya."

Just then Asavari called for a quick chat. "Have you heard Rehana is trying hard to make it to the Student Council next year? And Neville, too. By the way, don't you just hate Anshu's hair after she streaked it? How did her mom let her? I hear she's in big trouble with the prefects. Perhaps she thinks she's already a model... or Miss India."

Both the girls laughed and discussed their exam schedules.

"Prepared?" Sandhya enquired.

"Hardly," Asavari responded. "My entire history portion has to be revised... but I'm not worried. Dad has promised to set a few test papers. History is Dad's favourite subject even now. He's so sweet, he cancelled his Singapore trip because of my exams. It was a really important business meeting, but he said, 'Nothing is more important than your exams. I want to be there for you.'"

Sandhya said, "That's great. Now you can chill...
your dad's a good teacher. So is my dad... but he
doesn't get the time. Weekends are free... but I hate
to pile on. Mom and Dad work so hard throughout
the week... I hate to disturb them on a weekend."

Asavari said, "Come on Sandhya... that's what
parents are there for... you are being a bit too
considerate and good. If they're busy, so are we. If
they need to relax, so do we. Forget it... your dad is
such a whiz with numbers! He should give both of us
free tuitions in maths. And your mom can help us with
biology. Ugh. How I hate that subject. By the way...
guess what? I hear Mansi has a crush on that new
boy... what's his name? Anubhav... yeah... Anubhav.
Tall, thin, nice teeth."

Sandhya laughed. "Nice teeth? You're mad! You
notice such weird stuff. Anyway... I thought Mansi
had a crush on that other boy... Suraj?"

Asavari giggled. "Mansi's crushes change every
Friday – like Bollywood releases at theatres. Let's go
to a movie on Saturday... but will you be allowed?"

That was a standing joke between the girls.
Sandhya was rarely "allowed", while Asavari's dad

was far more liberal about her outings. It used to hurt Sandhya that her Dad didn't "allow" her to do all the stuff her friends' parents were so chilled out about. Sandhya wasn't "allowed" to wear certain clothes, chew gum, eat junk food, "misuse" phone calls, "waste time," sleep at "odd" hours, talk to "strange" boys, hang out late with friends, wear high heels or make-up, streak her hair, have her belly button pierced, get a permanent tattoo, experiment with halter-tops, wear red nail polish, "forget" her duties, remain seated when elders walked in…! Sometimes she felt like she was in a prison with all these strict rules. Not a single other friend had to deal with all this. As for going out at night?? Just forget it! Not even for a walk on the beach close by.

"It is dangerous," her mother would say.

"Out of the question," Dad would thunder.

"But why…?" Sandhya would argue.

"*Goondas*!" her father would reply shortly while Mom nodded in agreement. The way her parents went on and on about "*goondas*" it made Mumbai sound like a city filled with hard-core criminals waiting to pounce on young girls. How come her friends were not kept imprisoned in the same way?

She asked Mom once, and she'd replied in her characteristic calm way, "Each family has its own house rules… these are ours. I can't comment on other people's. Your father and I think about your safety before anything else. You'll have to trust us and respect our judgement, our long experience. Okay?"

Sandhya had lapsed into a sullen silence. There was nothing 'okay' about it. But did she have a choice? "Wait till I turn 18…," she had sworn to herself, "I'll show everybody."

Just then, Sandhya heard Bhaiya come in and hastily disconnected. Sandhya's endless chatathons with Asavari were an annoying, thorny issue between Bhaiya and her. It used to bug him no end to walk into the house and find his sister on the phone.

"Get off the line before I whack you one…," he'd shout, throwing his gear down on the bed and towering over Sandhya. It was no different this time.

Sid said, "I heard you gossiping… I know you disconnected just now – don't lie Sandhya!"

Sandhya silently beckoned him to come closer. "Sssh!" she said placing her finger on her lips. "Mom's home. And she's really mad at you!"

Sid looked startled. "Mad at me? What for? What have I done now?"

Sandhya whispered, "She knows you S-M-O-K-E!!"

She couldn't see Sid's expression since he had his back towards her. He didn't whirl around immediately. Nor did he instantly deny the charge.

He remained silent for a few seconds and then said abruptly, "Did you finish the crossword last night?"

Sandhya just stared at her brother. She was stupefied. "What are you talking about? Which crossword puzzle?"

Sid said vaguely, "You know... the one you do regularly... that idiotic one in the afternoon papers... pretty easy, actually."

Sandhya shook her head in disbelief. "Are you crazy or something? Didn't you hear what I just said?"

Sid paced the room and took an extra long drink of iced water. "I heard you... but let me just say this: You guys have got it all wrong."

Sandhya bit her lower lip. "What do you mean? Are you saying you don't? Smoke, that is?"

Sid didn't respond. He walked out saying, "I'll deal with Mom and Dad on this... tell them I've gone to Ashish's house to pick up some notes. As for that little twit, that little sneak Pia... wait till I get my hands on her. And the next time she needs ten bucks, I'll also fix her."

With that, Sid was gone, leaving Sandhya to wonder what that was about.

Sandhya was nervous and puzzled. What she needed was a musical break. And maybe a quick snack. *Bhelpuri? Samosa?* No, no, no. She rushed into her room to survey herself critically.

"Fat!" she said to her own image in the mirror. "F-A-T! I hate you."

Gauritai, who'd come in just then with a pile of neatly folded clothes, started laughing. "Fat? Who, you?? Then what am I – a she-elephant?"

Sandhya whirled around to face the woman who'd seen her since she was a few days old. "Tell me the truth – don't I look like a boiled potato?"

Gauritai laughed some more. "Not boiled. Fried," she teased.

Sandhya pulled a face and started helping Gauritai put all the freshly pressed clothes away. Gauritai grumbled away as she sorted out skirts, *kurtis*, T-shirts, nighties, socks, school uniforms, jeans and more jeans.

"That Pia baby is very untidy. Look at the mess she's made of her cupboard! When I complain to your mummy, Pia starts crying. But tell me – is this the way for a young girl to handle her belongings? One day, both of you will leave this house and go to your husband's home. There, you'll find a mother-in-law with a large stick in her hand. And if you disobey her, she will beat you up. Especially if you keep the house dirty and throw clothes all over the place. Why her? Even your husband will beat you."

Sandhya made clucking noises with her tongue. "It doesn't happen like that any more, Gauritai. Nobody beats a daughter-in-law."

Gauritai said firmly, "Of course it's still happening. Don't you watch TV serials? Every serial has the same story about *saas-bahu lafdas*. Tell me, are these TV people mad to show such things if they don't happen?"

Sandhya giggled. "But TV shows also have other things – do you believe everything you see?"

Gauritai shook her head. "No. Not everything. But I do know how a mother-in-law behaves. Why do you think I ran away to Mumbai from my village? I couldn't take her beatings any longer." And then she showed Sandhya an ugly scar on her left arm. "See this... that woman attacked me with a kitchen knife when I refused to massage her legs in the middle of the night. And then, when I fought her off, even my hopeless husband joined her in giving me a thrashing – that's when I decided to escape."

Sandhya listened to the old maid quietly. She'd heard the story before but never in such detail. She put her arm around Gauritai and wiped her tears with one of the hand towels from the pile.

"Don't cry, Gauritai. Now you are with us. You are safe. And your life is different. Forget the past. We all love you so much."

Gauritai nodded and blew her nose into the *pallav* of her sari. "God has been kind to me – very kind. I was so lucky to find a job in this house. Your mother is an angel. And your father's a good man. They've treated me well. See how generous Bhaiya is... he gives me money from his pocket money... he is more to me than my own worthless son."

Sandhya asked softly, "How is Bhiku? Where is he?"

Gauritai answered sadly, "Lying in some gutter... drunk. He will die the same way his father did, with a bottle in his hand. That is his fate and my destiny.

But let us not talk about such things. Tell me – what happened to Bhaiya? He seemed very upset. He left without eating the tasty noodles I'd made for him – his favourite – with those little-little corn pieces and mushrooms and all that. Did you fight with your brother?"

Sandhya shook her head emphatically. "Never!!" she retorted. "Why should I? I just told him what Pia has said to me... don't ask, I can't tell you. I can't tell anybody. It's terrible. I'm so ashamed."

Gauritai continued to tidy up the room in thoughtful silence. Finally she said, "It is none of my business, but I think I know what the problem is – you found out about... about... the cigarettes, right?"

Sandhya looked up sharply. "Right! But who told you??"

Gauritai chuckled. "Nobody told me... I have my own methods of finding out. After all, who cleans his room?? All the rooms?? Me!! Besides what do you think – don't I also have a nose, eyes, ears like you?"

Sandhya clung to Gauritai's arm and pleaded, "I implore you not to say anything to Mummy. She will be furious. As for Daddy, I don't want to be around when he finds out. Wait till I catch that Pia – it's all her fault. She's such a little sneak. A real *chaabi-master*."

Gauritai smiled indulgently. "She's still a baby... she doesn't understand. Why don't you go and practise your music now? Isn't it the day for your music teacher to come over for your lesson?"

Sandhya nodded and scampered off to get her gleaming, shining, amazing, dazzling synthesizer. Oh! How she loved it!! So much so, that she sometimes kissed the glossy surface. It was definitely Sandhya's most prized possession... after her precious Swatch watch, of course.

She still remembered that particular birthday...

Chapter Eleven

Bhaiya In Trouble

"Wow! I don't believe it, Dad!"

That had been Sandhya's reaction on her tenth birthday when her father had presented her with a synthesizer. Sandhya had been pleading for months. She'd even taken a vow – synthesizer on my birthday, please, please, please, God! You know how much I love music... I'll do anything – anything – if you get me a synthesizer. I'll study really, really hard. I'll do better in Math. I'll keep my room tidy. I won't fight with Pia. I'll show proper respect towards Bhaiya. I'll make sure Mom doesn't have to nag me about finishing my homework. But pleeeeeease God – my synthesizer... I really, really want it."

And there it was! Gleaming metallic grey and so beautiful.

Sandhya jumped up and down with joy, unable to contain her excitement. "You are the best Dad in the world," she cried, hugging him and kissing her mother. She noticed Pia staring at the scene from a corner of the room. Pia had tears in her eyes.

Sandhya had gone up to her and said, "Come on Pia... look... come and play it with me!"

Pia had turned away angrily saying, "Go away... I hate you... I hate that horrible noisy thing. I hate everybody. Nobody loves me... I know it. Everybody only loves you!"

Anu had rushed to her "baby" and comforted her by saying, "Guess what Dad's getting you for your birthday – just guess?"

But Pia had continued to cry and sulk for a week.

Sandhya thought of that momentous day as she began playing a few of her newly-learned sets. She also thought of how sweet Bhaiya had been. Seeing Pia's distress he'd hurried out of the house to the gift store nearby and come back with a bagful of cuddly soft toys. Plus, a toy guitar.

"There...," he'd said, handing everything over to

Pia. "Stop being a cry-baby – this is especially for you. Look... you can play 'Do Re Mi' on the guitar, just like this. And look at that cute Lion King listening to your strumming. See... the Pink Panther loves your song too. Come on, kid, wipe those big fat tears. You are losing too much salt... Unless you want Gauritai to add some of it to our food."

Everybody had laughed. Even Pia. Bhaiya was like that – so sweet and thoughtful when the occasion demanded it. And today he was going to get into deep trouble. Sandhya bit her lip with concern and wondered why and where he'd rushed away. She hoped it wasn't serious. Anyway, Mom always knew how to handle such situations.

And Mom adored Bhaiya, even if she denied he was her 'favourite.'

"What rubbish!" Anu used to exclaim, when teased about her *ladla beta*. "All my children are equal... there's no 'favourite' in my book."

Ha! Ha! Sandhya often laughed (in private, of course). Sometimes, Sandhya wondered whose favourite she was – Dad's? Not a chance. He doted on his "baby", that silly little Pia, who often lisped in his presence just to be cute. Not Mom's, for sure. She had Bhaiya. Then, whose? Sandhya wished she wasn't the middle child – she felt like a filling in a sandwich, crushed from two sides.

At other times she thought she was lucky, in a funny way. Because of her unique position, she got more respect from both Mom and Dad. They depended on her, trusted her. It was a great feeling, especially when they occasionally left town, keeping her in charge.

Pia would crib, "Don't think you're a queen or someone great just because Mom has told you to keep an eye on the house. In any case, if you try and bully me, I'll tell Dad – or get Bhaiya to beat you up."

Sandhya couldn't get Bhaiya's latest predicament out of her head. Sandhya remembered earlier occasions when Bhaiya had got into trouble with their parents. Once it was about trying to drive the family car and reversing it into the compound wall. That too, when he was just fifteen! Gosh! That had led to one big explosion at home. Bhaiya had been grounded for a week, without any pocket money.

"Misplaced" it, as he had kept insisting. "How careless," Ma had scolded. "Don't take these things so much for granted… we want to encourage you…

we want you to be a winner. But winners don't lose things… they value their sports gear. Does Leander Paes 'misplace' his racquet? Or Mahesh Bhupati lose his?"

Bhaiya had tried hard to defend himself, but the truth was, he had been negligent. Dad had also blown a fuse and told him to make do with his old racquet.

"But Dad, it is from another era," Bhaiya had protested. "Everybody will laugh at me… even the coach."

"Too bad!" Dad had said. "You should have thought of all this before leaving yours on a bench somewhere."

That had been that. Sandhya knew her parents were very clear and very firm when it came to certain issues. Which is why they'd refused to get her a mobile phone for a long long time. And when she did get one, it was her mother's old phone – such an old-fashioned, dated and basic model that Sandhya felt embarrassed to use it ! Asavari had laughed aloud and said teasingly, "It is a dinosaur… a prehistoric cell. Wow! Let us keep it in a museum!"

Well… Bhaiya's newest problem was different. He had broken the family's cardinal rule – 'No Smoking!' She went over the entire smoking scenario several times. If Bhaiya had taken to smoking she would definitely have known about it – how can you hide the awful stink? Yes, Bhaiya's sweatshirts did smell of smoke sometimes, but whenever she'd asked him about it, he'd dismissed it saying, "Oh... I was at the club... some of the guys were smoking."

And, of course, she'd believed him! Sandhya never doubted her brother's word. Bhaiya was honest and frank – why would he lie to her? And if he did indeed smoke in his room, Gauritai would've told Mom about finding cigarette butts, lighters or matches.

No, no, Bhaiya would never get into such a foul habit. After all, tobacco was a topic that had been discussed at home so frequently, especially by Mom who would talk about people suffering from all sorts of horrible lung, throat and mouth diseases because of smoking and eating *gutkha*.

Sandhya was worried and upset. She decided to write a letter to Bhaiya telling him how concerned she was. Sandhya often did that with Mom, Dad and Bhaiya. She would write long notes stating her feelings when she felt she couldn't talk face-to-face with someone, for whatever reason. Yes, that's exactly what she'd do.

So, she rushed to her desk and pulled out her 'best' letter paper – the one she hoarded possessively for really special people and for really special occasions.

She began:

Dearest, Darlingest Bhaiya,

I am so-o-o-o scared. You know how Mom and Dad and all of us feel about smoking. And Mom has told you how dangerous it is. I just want you to tell the truth – if you do smoke, say it. And if you don't, say that too. We are family. We love each other, right? We are there to correct each other, too, right? Nobody will be angry if you say 'sorry', and promise to give it up. But Bhaiya, Mom and Dad will really freak out if you deny it and they find out that you were lying. I know you will do the right thing. I know you won't let us down. Whatever it is, I'll be there for you. So will Pia. For sure. So... please, please, don't get mad if I've said anything stupid, okay? I don't want you to get into trouble, that's all. Okay, Bhaiya. Take care. I hope your pocket money doesn't get cut!

Bye,

Chutki

Sandhya smiled when she saw the way she'd signed off. "Chutki" was Sid's special name for her. The one he'd given her when she was two years old. It had stuck. But it was only Sid who was allowed to call her "Chutki". Each time Pia tried, Sandhya would shut her up. Particularly when Pia taunted her.

"See, see, even your pet name is dumb. What's "Chutki"? It sounds so stupid! Poor you. First Mom and Dad call you "Sandhya" – chhhee – and then Bhaiya calls you "Chutki". If I had such stupid names, I would definitely kill myself."

Pia was forever threatening to "kill" herself for every small thing. By now, Sandhya reasoned, she should've been "dead" hundred times over. Pest!! Anyway, she folded Bhaiya's letter neatly and went into his bedroom to place it on his pillow. She loved going into Bhaiya's room; it always smelled of pleasant colognes and after-shave lotions (Bhaiya had quite a neat collection).

Normally, Sandhya went there looking for CDs (Bhaiya had a neat collection of those, as well). But today, she found herself sniffing around – literally. She felt bad – like a sneak. But she was genuinely worried about Bhaiya. So, she shut the door softly and decided to investigate for herself. Any tell-tale signs? Any forgotten ash? Butts? Matchboxes? Lighters?

She opened Bhaiya's book-crammed cupboard – and nearly fell down when a mountain of books descended on her. Oh God! Bhaiya's book mania was too much – he was constantly adding titles to his precious "library", and now there was just no space to stack all his favourites. She scrambled to put them back into their rightful places – Bhaiya hated anybody (even her!) rummaging through his "things". And he was particularly possessive about his books.

Oops, she'd stuck one in upside down! He'd know for sure – she was dead! Just as she'd finished shoving the last one into its cramped slot, the door burst open – and there he was – Bhaiya, himself.

"What the hell are you doing in my room?" he yelled. "And why are you touching my books? I've told you hundreds of times to stay out. Now – go! Out, out, out."

Sandhya, who'd been so startled by the "intrusion" she'd actually jumped back a few paces, looked pleadingly at her brother.

"Please, Bhaiya don't be angry... I was only trying to help you... I don't want you to get caught... Mom's so upset... I've never seen her like that...," Sandhya cried.

Sid exploded, "What's wrong with all of you? Have you gone totally mad? What's all this nonsense, huh? Come on, tell me."

Just then Pia walked in, her face alight with curiosity. The room was suddenly silent, as the three of them stared at one another, wondering what would happen next...

Chapter Twelve

Two Problems

Back in her room, Sandhya agonised. Oh God! Mom would have to deal with two major problems: her own horrible secret, and Bhaiya's smoking. For a moment, Sandhya felt sorry for Mom. But in a jiffy, she switched back to feeling sorry for herself. Life was so difficult these days, Sandhya thoughtfully concluded. Not just for her, but all her friends. And their friends.

Even adults were in deep trouble. It just wasn't fair. There was too much trouble in the world. And how did God expect everyone to deal with it? She had several bones to pick with God. But she would do so at the Satyanarayan Puja next week. Oh-oh. She'd almost forgotten!

The Puja's date clashed with her class party. She hadn't dared tell Mom so far. Sandhya knew Mom would never allow her to skip the annual puja at home. But Sandhya desperately wanted to go to the class party – her first. And that too, the one that officially allowed the boys from the neighbouring school to attend – provided they bought tickets, wore appropriate clothes and behaved themselves!

Sandhya chuckled when she recalled some of the stories she'd heard down the years. How Pandu, the school peon, would chase the naughtier ones out of the school gate, brandishing a big stick – or how Mrs. Iyer, her headmistress would watch the boys like a hawk, from her special perch in the school hall. Sandhya definitely didn't want to miss her first "mixed" party – why – she'd got her outfit organised weeks ago.

Though secretly Sandhya was dying to wear a "designer outfit", a trendy *kurti*, like the one Rani Mukherjee wore, or Kareena, she knew Ma wouldn't hear of it. Once she'd tried saying something about buying an outfit from a pricey boutique in South Mumbai; Ma had dismissed her request within seconds.

"What nonsense – how can you wear something so ridiculously expensive? Twenty thousand rupees? No way! Do you know a young underprivileged child from the slums can get an education for that much money? It can feed an entire family for a year!" Sandhya had stared at her toes.

"But Asavari's dad took her there for her birthday," she'd started saying.

Ma had held up her hand. "Enough, I would never encourage you to waste money on such things. I don't want to comment on Asavari's dad - that's his business."

Sandhya frowned to herself. Why was Ma so strict? So sensible? Sometimes, Sandhya referred to Ma as "Hitler". Dad was easier to *patao*, especially when it came to "girlie" things like colouring hair.

"It's okay," he'd told Ma, in his good-humoured, weekend-voice way. "*Fashion hai*, these days."

Ma had fixed him with a stunned stare. "It may be in fashion. But that was my final word on it."

At fourteen ("nearly fifteen" as she always clarified), Sandhya was fairly tall ("But I want to be still taller," she used to insist) and athletic in appearance, thanks to the netball, throwball and swimming practice Ma had started her off on since the age of nine. Or, as Dad preferred to put it, "You have taken after my side of the family – *faujis* and sportspeople."

Sandhya looked at herself closely for the hundredth time. She was never entirely happy about the image in the mirror. "I wish my hair was straighter – like Ravina's. And I wissssshh Ma would allow me to colour it at least during the holidays."

Sandhya didn't like her waistline and hips too much either. "Twenty-six inches… soooooo fat,' she'd moan, drawing her breath in.

Then looking at her hips wail, "I'll never get into my old jeans again, I'll never look like Shilpa Shetty… or Britney…."

Sandhya's obsession with her figure had become a family joke. Bhaiya in particular, teased her incessantly.

"Hi Kareena," he'd greet her.

Why couldn't Mom understand that every young person loved such clothes? Each time she watched TV, she'd look longingly at all those models… how fashionable they looked in sequinned, rainbow-coloured *kurtis*… compared to those outfits, her denim skirt looked… looked ugh. Not totally ugh – but she really, really wanted an amazing *kurti*. Maybe she'd ask Dad. Sometimes, he was more generous... Or... Or... the halter top. Or... Or... no... she loved tubes and spaghettis... but Mom would flip if she as much as suggested those. Naturally that bratty Pia was jealous. And naturally, Pia had hated it. But Bhaiya had said the cute denim skirt suited her. And he was the one who'd bought her the sporty T-shirt to go with it. Sandhya had surveyed herself in the mirror countless times wearing her new clothes.

But now, the puja date had been finalised by the pundit, and it coincided with the class party. There was no way Mom would allow the children to miss the puja – it was an annual ritual that mattered a lot to Mom and Dad. A ritual that went back several years when Mom herself was a little girl. Sandhya loved the puja and looked forward to participating in it. But this year she was torn between the two – party or puja? Definitely, the party!

Sandhya came out of her daydream with a start. What was that rustling noise?

Chapter Thirteen

Cool Coffee

Sandhya rushed to the window. Oh, it was only a branch of her favourite tree chafing against the sill. A few days earlier, she'd stopped some vagrants from chopping down the branches.

"But we need wood to burn," they'd shouted defiantly.

"Don't cut my tree!" Sandhya had screamed before rushing down and physically preventing them from hacking it. The commotion had attracted the attention of neighbours and several passers-by. The miscreants had fled, leaving their axes behind. Sandhya's timely intervention had saved this one beautiful, adult gulmohar tree – but how many others had been senselessly chopped down?

Sandhya gazed at the pale green, velvety new leaves fluttering prettily in the breeze. How happy and carefree they looked! She wished she could feel the same way herself. But with the weight of the awful secret getting her down, Sandhya wore a perpetually troubled look. Yesterday, Mom had noticed it. So had Dad.

"Anything wrong?" both had asked over dinner. Sandhya had been quick to deny it. But she knew her parents had sensed her anxiety. Later, Pia had hissed, "Why don't you just tell them the truth? That way, it won't be your problem – it will become theirs!"

Sandhya had shut her up with a fierce look. And picked up the phone to talk to her other best friend, Priya. She was away at tuitions. God! It was impossible to find someone to talk to when you most needed to. Everybody was busy these days. Including Priya. Too busy to chat or help.

Anyway, the main thing now was to get the pundit to change the puja date, without Mom finding out. But how? The family *pujari* was a tough old man, who knew so many *mantras*, Sandhya's head would reel. She'd watched him during all those pujas, as he came a few hours prior to the slated time and arranged all the puja *saaman* – fragrant jasmines, red hibiscus, tender banana leaves, garlands of marigolds, *kumkum*, *chandan*, rice grains, pure ghee, turmeric powder, *dhoop*. Then the *diyas* would be carefully prepared, while *agarbattis* were arranged around the small *chaurang* (four-legged stool). Sandhya's Mom loved the occasion and insisted on everybody wearing traditional, festive clothes. Even Dad donned a *dhoti* for the puja.

And Gauritai always sang during the *aarti*, clad in her best saree. Sandhya bit her lip, thinking hard. Tricking the *pujari* would be really hard. He was too smart. But she would come up with something convincing when the time was right; the school party was tooooo important to miss!!

Because, if she missed the party, she'd really be missing something. And Sandhya had been dreaming about that one evening for an entire year. She would get to dance with a guy, there would be a professional DJ mixing the music, and who knows, maybe Akshi would turn up too! Sandhya blushed at the very thought of Akshay. Of course, he was cute, all the girls thought so. Maybe he knew he was cute, too.

So what? If he did show up, Sandhya knew she'd never get to speak to him, much less dance. But, at least they'd be sharing the same space. He'd probably ignore her totally. Sandhya had heard he had a girl-friend from his own snob-school. They were often seen driving around in her fancy car. He'd also been spotted at a Barista near his home, buying her a café latté and a brownie. Sandhya did feel a twinge of jealousy visualising the scene, but she knew her own feelings for Akshi were so deep and sincere, that she was willing to accept him in totality. And his girlfriend Natasha was really, really, hot.

Much as Sandhya hated to admit it, she was horribly, miserably, terribly jealous of 'Nattie, the Hottie' not only because she was Akshi's girl, but because she had major attitude. Nattie was just so super-confident about everything, it gave all the girls an instant complex. Priya and Sandhya spent ("wasted") hours discussing Nattie. Nattie and her fake accent ("Is it Colaba or California?"). Nattie and her fancy clothes ("Linking Road dressed up to look like Los Angeles"). Nattie and her dad's amazing car ("Okay, so he drives a BMW, big deal"). Nattie on Facebook. God, didn't she have better things to do? Imagine uploading twenty pictures of herself on a daily basis. What a show-off! And some of them were with Akshi! Nattie, it was agreed, bugged the whole school. Sigh. But she was Akshi's 'Chosen One'. And that was that.

There were times Sandhya wasn't at all sure she liked being a teenager or even if she liked her family. Somehow they just didn't seem as "cool" as the members of her friend's families.

"Cool" – not Sandhya's word at all. More Pia's. A word that actually irritated Sandhya. She'd often scream at Pia: "OK stop all your "cool-cool" talk, you sound like such a wannabe."

Sigh. Being fourteen (almost fifteen) was such a pain sometimes.

Sandhya looked at the denim skirt again. And the T-shirt. It was okay - just about. But she'd have given anything for that amazing top she'd seen on Katz – her new best friend forever. Katz was lucky. Her father worked for a foreign airline. Her mother was a travel writer who was sent to exotic destinations by various magazines. Katz rarely wore "Indian" clothes. Nearly everything in her wardrobe was imported. All the girls envied Katz, especially when they saw her wearing the latest fashions from London or New York. Anyway, Sandhya knew she wouldn't be able to push Ma or Dad for anything too expensive.

She could almost hear Ma say, "Nonsense! Seven thousand rupees for a flimsy skirt! It's not about the money, Sandhya. It is crazy for such a young person to wear clothes that cost as much as the salary of someone like our clerk, Sonali."

Hmm... Sandhya stared dubiously at her denim skirt for the nth time. Naah! It wouldn't do. She'd think of something else... Something much cooler. But for now, she had to complete her journal. Ugh! Like she cared a jot about Chandragupta Maurya's empire. All she really, really cared about right now was an alternative to that denim skirt. And of course, the streaks she was dying to get in her long, dark hair like Natasha.

Nattie was the star performer in Shiamak Davar's troupe. In fact, she was so good, she'd been included in the back-up dancers' group that had gone to perform at some Film Awards in Dubai. Imagine! She had danced with Salman Khan! And met Ranbir! Sandhya found herself feeling really, really jealous, especially because she knew that Nattie must have met Aishwarya at the show, too... maybe even talked to her!! Sandhya adored "Ash" and didn't miss a single film of hers. It was Ash who had indirectly pushed Sandhya into taking dance lessons. Of course, Ma and Dad had wanted her to learn classical Indian dance from the time she was five years old. But it was after watching Madhuri Dixit and Ash in *Devdas* during the spectacular *Dola Re* dance sequence that Sandhya had made up her mind and enrolled. Her friends teased her for days, saying, "How silly you look… who learns Indian dancing these days? Look at you… everyone will laugh. We're going to salsa classes like everybody else."

Sandhya turned away from gazing at her favourite tree. She knew she had to work on her Chemistry portion – but how she hated it! Why did God invent chemistry? Why did anybody have to know how gases reacted with each other? Who cared? Except her chem-teacher, class teacher and headmistress. And Mom, of course.

Sandhya reluctantly opened her textbook and tried to concentrate on all those equations and formulae, which actually looked like ants crawling across the page. Soon, Bhaiya would return. Mom and Dad, too. Sandhya had to come up with a convincing strategy to postpone the puja. There was no way she was going to miss the class party – just no way. She thought of the denim skirt again. A little tight on the hips, but she'd lose weight. If, by any remote chance, Akshay looked in her direction at all that evening, she wanted to make pretty sure he'd see a "slim and cool" chick – like Nattie. No, someone much better than Nattie. But for that Sandhya would need to team the skirt with that strappy top – but Ma would never hear of it.

She gave up studying and went to her cupboard. She threw it open. God! Which top should she wear??

The persistent ring of her cell phone dragged Sandhya away from her wardrobe. It was 'A' sounding excited.

"Listen, Dad's allowed me a treat because I babysat Duggu all morning. Let's go to Barista for a coffee, na."

More than happy to forget her clothing woes, Sandhya agreed promptly. Half an hour later, the two friends trooped arm-in-arm into the happening neighbourhood coffee shop. As the door swung behind them, Sandhya's jaw dropped and she froze in her tracks. Standing at the counter looking really super-cool in his Levi's and sporty tee was Akshay. And seated at a table close by, was his girlfriend looking trendy in a short denim skirt.

Asavari pinched Sandhya. "Wake up and move.

Don't behave like a moron. Act normal."

As casually as possible, they walked to the counter where Akshay stood. Asavari cleared her throat and addressed the attendant.

"Excuse me, two cold coffees please, with chocolate cream."

Two coffees in hand, Akshay had meanwhile turned to move towards his table. Of course, he spotted Sandhya.

"Oh, hi Sandy! We meet again. How are things?" Akshay smiled.

"W…W…wonderful. Gr…gr…great," stuttered Sandhya, wishing she had better control over her tongue.

"Is your nanaji better?" asked Akshay.

Sandhya nodded in reply and after a split second asked, "And your masi?"

"She's good," said Akshay.

Then bobbing his head towards the table where his girlfriend sat, he said, "Gotta go now. See you. And by the way," he added with a wink, "glad to see you took my tip about the hairstyle."

As Akshay walked away, Sandhya felt her heart was beating so loudly, everyone at the coffee shop could hear it. Their cold coffees arrived and the two friends sat at a table not far from the one Akshay occupied.

"Sandy? Did he call you Sandy?" Asavari giggled.

Sandhya nodded. "What else could I do? Sandhya's such a dumb name."

Asavari rolled her eyes dramatically, exclaiming, "What if he finds out your real name?"

So startled was Sandhya at this trend of thought, she promptly spilt her coffee – some on the table and most on her shirt-front.

Asavari's loud yelp, "Oh, no!" attracted all the attention Sandhya could have done without.

Red-faced with embarrassment, the two fled the coffee shop.

Chapter Fourteen

Too Many Secrets

Pia doubled up with laughter when she overheard Sandhya discussing the class party over the phone with Kreetika, the nerdy class monitor. What would Kreets know about parties and DJ's and boys and Beyonce? Rihanna? Fergie?? Why waste time talking to her?

Pia pointed to herself and said loudly, "If you need advice, ask me – I'm the expert."

Sandhya scowled at her kid sister's cheekiness and continued the conversation. The entire class was supposed to participate in the party, one way or the other. It was their responsibility to sell as many tickets, as many game stall coupons and as many lucky dip vouchers as possible. After all, the money collected would go towards a good cause – a shelter for underprivileged children.

Most girls from Sandhya's batch were very involved in the project, but a few were being difficult. Kreets had enlisted Sandhya's help to ensure the difficult ones did not disrupt the party.

Sandhya said, "I know Pinkie is the main problem. Don't worry, I'll tackle her. She feels she has not been given any importance. Why don't we give her a stall to handle on her own? I know what – let's make her the fortune-telling gypsy with the crystal ball! She'd love that and she'd also be very good at it. Once Pinkie agrees, the others won't be a problem – trust me."

Pia pulled faces and kept distracting Sandhya. At one point, Sandhya chucked a pillow at Pia, who while trying to dodge it, fell off the bed and bumped her head against the edge. Pia began to bawl at full volume, much to Sandhya's annoyance.

"How many times have I told you not to listen to my conversations? You are such a pain! Get out right now. This is important... just go!" But Pia stayed put on the floor, yelling and screaming for ice.

"Stop howling like a baby," Sandhya said, while Kreets held on. Finally, an exasperated Gauritai stuck her head into the room to say, "Fighting again, you two? I don't know what sort of warring stars you were born under – your poor mother must have done something bad in her past life to give birth to such girls – forever fighting. Your *kundalis* are crossed! *Hey Bhagwan*! Never have I seen two sisters who fight as much."

Pia demanded ice, bandages, a doctor.

"Shut up, you little twit, or I'll whack you hard," Sandhya threatened. "Here I am, discussing something important with Kreets. Why don't you mind your own business and just stay out of my hair? Can't you see I'm worried?"

Through her feigned sobs, Pia looked at Sandhya and taunted, "Yeah? Worried about what? Akshi ignoring you? Clumsy, coffee-spilling clown that you are!"

Sandhya rushed towards Pia with her hand raised. At that moment Sid walked in with a big, broad grin on his face. Sandhya whirled around, hand still in the air and exclaimed, "Bhaiya! Help! Pia is driving me nuts – I was going to slap her just now."

Sid came and punched Sandhya playfully and gave her a jaunty high-five as Pia asked cheekily, "Big smile, huh, Bhaiya? How come? And what's with all this *pyar-vyar*? Come on, confess... you did it again didn't you? Bhaiya will be killed by Mom and Dad... Bhaiya is dead. And so is this *bhoot*... Didi, you are dead too. Don't think I'm going to keep both your secrets forever... if you try and slap me, I'll phone and tell Mom."

Sandhya let out a long breath and leaned against her brother. "Too many secrets these days... I'm so tired, Bhaiya... let's both tell Mom and Dad the truth... what's the point? How long can we hide it?"

Sid grinned some more. "I have no secret, frankly, so, I'm cool. But hey – what's this about your secret? Let's hear it."

Sandhya threw a warning look in Pia's direction, as if to stop her from opening her mouth. "Just shut up, okay? Let me tell Bhaiya myself. But first, I want Bhaiya to tell us about all this smoking business."

Sid sat on their bed and patted the place next to him, "Come on girls – sit here... but first, let's get Gauritai to make us some yummy popcorn and *garam masala chai*... go on, Sandhya... organise it, fast."

Sandhya turned to Pia, "You do it."

Pia argued, "No, you do it. Why should I keep

doing everything? Stop bullying me."

Sid strode to the door and yelled, "G-A-U-R-I-T-A-I."

Turning to his sisters, he muttered, "Useless," under his breath.

Sandhya glared at Pia and said, "See... now Bhaiya is irritated. All because of you. I hate you."

Pia pulled a face. "Ditto – Ditto."

Pia caught her own reflection in the mirror and made her 'cute' face. Pia was always pulling cute faces much to her family's annoyance. "Stop it… stop acting all the time," Sandhya would admonish her. "Don't think you are in the movies."

Pia was crazy about Bollywood and its stars. This was another problem. Sid, at eighteen, had no time to indulge his kid sister's constant demands to take her to the movies. And Sandhya had zero interest in going to the movies with that brat, Pia. Their mom and dad were too busy to take time off for such pursuits. Which left Pia, Gauritai and their jet-black cocker spaniel Zorro to sit in front of the TV screen watching old reruns or music channels playing the latest songs or the dance reality shows with celebrity couples shaking a leg. Gauritai also had another weakness – TV soaps in Marathi. And she blushed each time she saw her favourite hero on the small screen. The children giggled over her secret "crush". But Mom thoroughly disapproved of such jokes.

Pia loved to dance and was good at picking up new steps. While Sid indulged Pia, her incessant humming and dancing bugged Sandhya. "You look really stupid trying to do these filmi *jhatkas*. Be your age."

Gauritai would promptly intervene. "Leave her alone, Sandhya, she's just having fun… what's so bad about dancing?"

On the rare occasions Mom walked in and caught Pia behaving like Shilpa Shetty, she'd frown slightly then smile and say, "Pia… why don't you join a good Bharat Natyam class? If you are so keen on dancing, take lessons in classical dance."

If Mom only knew! Pia's secret dream was to grow up in a hurry and join Bollywood. But only Zorro and Gauritai knew her plans.

Bhaiya's tea arrived. He took long sips, demanded some more and then addressed the girls solemnly. He was tall, athletic and good-looking with broad shoulders and eyes that were often described as 'melting chocolates'. His sisters adored him – as did several other girls from his class.

Sid was very much a ladies' man (as his dad described him indulgently) but he was also a guy's guy since he'd been voted Super Achiever by his classmates in the popular boarding school for boys where he had studied. After finishing school and getting into a college in Mumbai, Sid had lost a little of his intense focus, a fact that worried his parents. His grades had dropped, and he seemed more than a little distracted.

"It's normal," Dad explained to Mom and the girls when the first term reports came in. "Sid will take time to settle down – he's been away from home and in a protected, boarding school environment for many years. Don't worry about him – he'll be fine." Mom understood that Sid was going through a strange phase. And she had a name for it – Girls.

All that female attention may have been a bit too sudden, but Sid was definitely loving every minute of it. "How cool am I?" he'd say to his sisters before stepping out in the evenings. They would stare at him critically and tease, "So… who are you seeing this week? Sapna, Rina or Tina?"

Naturally, they picked up most of his calls too, and eavesdropped on as many conversations as they could. This time, they knew Sid had something serious to discuss.

"Look.... I want you to know one thing – I am not a liar. And I keep my promises. When Mom and Dad had expressed their views on the ill-effects of smoking to me, I was only 12 years old. At that time, I'd wondered why they were lecturing me. That too, about smoking! I didn't smoke. Nobody I knew in my class smoked... I never wanted to smoke! But I heard them out and forgot all about it. Then, when I had just joined junior college, some of my friends started puffing – just as an experiment. That's when I remembered what Mom and Dad had told me.

"But I was also tempted. One day, Samir said, 'Come on, *yaar*, have a drag ... just one drag. It won't kill you...' So, just to show him I wasn't afraid, I had a drag. Soon, I was having these casual drags everyday. And feeling terrible. My friends said it was okay – everybody smoked. I knew they were wrong, but I wanted to prove to them that I wasn't some nerdy guy.

"Anyway, one day, I found myself waking up at night with a terrible cough – a dry cough. It wouldn't stop. Mom must have heard me – she came to the room. Maybe she suspected I'd been smoking but she kept quiet, gave me a glass of water and told me to go back to sleep. But that night I got scared – really scared. And I promised myself I would quit. And I did!

That's the truth. Trust me. If you find matchbooks or even cigarette packs, you have to believe me when I say those are old discarded ones.

"Sometimes, when Samir and some of the guys come over, they do smoke. I've told them this is a smoke-free house – but they still light up. You know how it is – but my mind is made up. I'm going to tell Mom and Dad exactly what I just told you. I'm sure they'll understand. What do you think?"

Sandhya and Pia looked at each other. They weren't sure how to react. Bhaiya was being honest – that much they knew without doubt. But what would Mom say? And Dad? Both would feel let down, at least a little. Both would feel disappointed that Bhaiya had not paid enough attention to their warnings. But at least Bhaiya had not held back anything. And he deserved to be forgiven.

Spontaneously, the girls rushed to hug their brother. And tell him, it was okay. Everything would be fine. These things happened. Mom would be hurt and upset. But she would also understand. And Dad? Well, Dad would be a tougher nut to crack. Hmmm. Strategy needed! They decided to put their heads together and come up with a good plan!

Chapter Fifteen

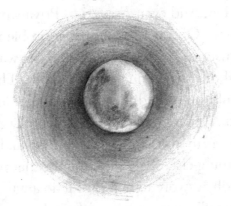

Moon Talk

But Sandhya continued to be troubled. Bhaiya's problem would be solved somehow. It was simpler. And Bhaiya had already decided how he would tackle Mom and Dad. Sandhya was petrified, since she knew she'd soon be found out, anyway. And then what would she do? Where would she hide? Oh God! The shame and the horror of it all. Sandhya was aware that she had very little time. There was a lot of quick thinking still to be done. And nobody to turn to for advice. Aaah – why not Nani or Nana? They always had solutions for everything. But... but... would they understand? Would they be shocked? Would they hate her forever?

Sandhya decided to sleep over it. No use asking that silly Pia. And even Asavari or Priya wouldn't be of any help. Oh no! This horrible problem had to crop up just now, of all times. Just as she was getting excited about the annual school party. The whole thing would be ruined if Mom and Dad found out before that. And then she would have to stay grounded for at least six months, maybe an entire year. But more than anything else, she'd have to miss that party! No way! Sandhya swore to herself. I'll do anything to go to the "social" – even run away from home and hide, if I have to. Yes – that sounded like a good plan. But running away wasn't easy.

Run where? How? Who'd keep her, feed her? Sandhya postponed thinking about annoying details like that. Let Mom and Dad deal with Bhaiya and his confession first, she told herself. Mine can wait, till after the party. Once the big night was over, she didn't care about the consequences – she was ready to face them and take whatever punishment her parents decided to mete out. Sandhya's mind was made up. The plan was on. Now all that was needed was to keep that pesky, nosy Pia out of her hair for the next few days. And 'Detective' Gauritai, of course.

Those two were capable of anything, even shameless spying and snooping. Sandhya would have to be very careful about her movements. And, of course, her phone calls. She vowed to keep absolutely mum. This was one plan she wouldn't share with a soul – not even Asavari and Priya, her chief advisers and trusted friends.

Sandhya ran into the bathroom to share her thrill with her own image in the mirror for the fifth time that day. "Yesssss!" she exulted, "Yesssss!!" From the corner of her eye, she noticed Pia staring at her.

"Crazy! You've finally lost it! I always knew you were mad. Now I know you are fully mad! Wait till I tell all your friends that you talk to yourself in the loo. See how they'll laugh at you. Better still – I'll let the whole world know on the Internet – that way Akshi won't even look at you at your stupid Social. In any case, you don't even have a proper outfit and all your friends will look much better. And… and… you've got a big, fat, red ugly pimple on your forehead. Pimple face, pimple face! You cannot use make-up. Nor will you be allowed to stay out late like the others. And Dad will flip out if you tell him that there may be beer at the party. Don't lie. The boys hide it in their cola. Mom won't let you go – everybody knows that. And what will you do with your dumb hair? I know what – why don't you take some advice from Malice Mehta – ha ha!"

Sandhya's enthusiasm collapsed as she stared angrily at Pia. She decided to keep quiet for the moment. Her plan was far too important and she didn't want to lose her concentration – not now.

So Sandhya said sweetly to Pia, "Oh... please don't tell anyone. I was just rehearsing for my class play. I hope I get the main part. It's a really cool play this year. I'm so excited."

Pia looked at her for a minute or so in silence, as if assessing her words.

"Liar!" she said finally. "Your play got over last term. You are fibbing. Tell me the truth, or else I'll tell Mom your secret this evening – the minute she comes home."

Sandhya's face crumpled. She knew she would have to deal with Mom very soon. And she hated the thought of Pia holding a sword over her head like this. There was just one way to deal with it. And Sandhya decided the risk was worth it. "Fine. Go ahead and sneak. Tell Mom everything. I don't care. But remember if you do that you will lose my trust forever."

Pia thought about it in silence. While Sandhya held her breath, Pia abruptly left the room. Sandhya heaved a huge sigh of relief and picked up her Maths workbook tiredly. Twenty sums. Hateful. But she'd have to tackle them somehow. And that Science portion she'd been putting off – yes, that too. But till then she would dream of her "look" for the social. And tell the moon all about it!

Sandhya had a special relationship with the moon. It had started when she was around five years old and miserable. Her pet dog, (the one before Zorro) Puddles, had died, and Sandhya had been inconsolable for days. No amount of sympathy could comfort her. She felt alone and very, very sad. Puddles had been her steady companion since her birth. He was a handsome, noble Labrador. He used to "talk" to her. And she, of course talked incessantly to Puddles, especially after a scolding. Besides, Mom's attention in those days used to be divided between Bhaiya and Baby Pia. Everybody expected Sandhya to look after herself. And nobody knew just how lonely she felt at times. Nobody, except Puddles.

The day he died in her lap still remained the saddest day of Sandhya's life. That night as she lay in bed, she saw the moon, as if for the first time. It was a full-moon night. And it looked so wise and kind, Sandhya stared at its full face beseechingly. "Please, dear moon, please help me find Puddles in the sky, wherever he may be. I will make you my friend for life."

And the moon had responded with a soft reassurance that had touched Sandhya's heart profoundly and permanently. While staring at its glorious face, Sandhya had seen a tender smile conveying understanding, love and kindness, all at once.

She knew at that moment that the moon was definitely listening and she had made the moon her trusted companion. Even on those nights when the moon stayed away from showing its pretty face to the world, Sandhya knew it was looking out for her from its secret hiding place. And her conversations never ceased. Nobody knew about her special relationship with the moon, not even her best friend at the time. Sandhya remembered the sheer magic of gazing at the moon's image in a water-filled *thali* that Gauritai had shown her once. "The moon is dancing for you," Gauritai had said, moving the *thali* gently from side-to-side. And Sandhya had been entirely captivated to see her "friend" swaying gently, with tiny ripples of water creasing its luminous face.

Today, too, Sandhya was in the mood to tell the moon all about her problems with Pia, her worry about Bhaiya, and of course, her secret. But before that, she needed to tackle those twenty horrible sums and finish the science chapter. Oh! How I hate my studies, Sandhya groaned, biting her lip in frustration.

There was also the other thing Mom was soon going to discover. Sandhya had bunked a few tuitions. And fibbed to the tutor about her absences. She hated her Hindi *masterji*, with his thick black nostril hair and nasal accent. And she was scared of the strict Science "ma'am", who thought nothing of "tapping" her students across their knuckles with a hard ruler.

The English teacher was okay, but my God, how weird she was, in her strange little "frocks" with roses and pansies embroidered on the collar. And that peculiar haircut which was so unruly, the curls flew all over her face as she read endless passages from *Macbeth*.

Sandhya felt a little sorry for poor Ms.Pocha. She looked so frail and ate so little. Her wrists were like a child's, and her skin like parchment. Nobody ever saw her eat or drink anything, even in the staff room. She carried no lunch, no snacks, only a large bottle of water.

"Maybe she doesn't like food," others volunteered.

Meanwhile, Sandhya couldn't stop herself from staring at Ms.Pocha's exposed ankles, which looked so alarmingly thin. Sandhya often wondered how they could bear even scrawny Ms.Pocha's weight.

It didn't matter at all. For Ms.Pocha was an absolute angel who had opened Sandhya's eyes, ears and mind to the splendours of Shelley and Keats at a time when girls her age were drooling over Barbie dolls and Britney's hits. Ms.Pocha's lilting diction had entranced Sandhya, even if she'd been too shy to reveal her admiration for Ms.Pocha to her classmates.

Sandhya remembered a small but telling incident. When a class bully, the horrid Amy, had succeeded in reducing Ms.Pocha to tears by mimicking her cruelly in front of the entire class, it was Sandhya who had shot to her feet and said, "Stop it Amy! You are being mean. And you know what – it isn't even funny."

Amy had glared at Sandhya, while the rest of the class had been stunned into silence.

And then, Amy had backed off. Just like that. Ms. Pocha had excused herself discreetly and with great delicacy. The class had stared in horror at the bird-like teacher rushing off to the staff room. Sandhya had withdrawn, leaving her friends to tackle Amy.

'How could you? What's your problem? You are sick!' they had screamed, as Amy looked defiantly at her classmates, stuck her chin out and said, "Good for you, you little *chamchis*. Ms.Pocha is a yucky teacher – I hate her and her silly, fake accent. Poor thing. She's so pathetic! Born in the wrong country and speaking the wrong language, too. Give me a break!"

Ms.Pocha had taken sick leave for a week. The next time she entered their class, the girls cheered and greeted her with a bunch of flowers. On the board, Sandhya had written: *Welcome Back Ms. Pocha*, in coloured chalk. Amy had sat in the last row, silent and sullen, as the class listened to Ms.Pocha's whispery recitation of *An Ode to a Nightingale*.

The moon was not in a sympathetic mood as Sandhya poured her heart out that night. On the contrary, the expression on the moon's face was distinctly disapproving. Sandhya wondered whether to turn to her heavily-guarded diary instead. It was her most private possession. But she wasn't in the mood to write. She wasn't in the mood to do anything – not even fight with Pia.

All she actually had on her mind was the school social. And, of course, Akshi. Sandhya's face reddened and her ears turned warm just at the thought of him. For the hundredth time she went over her encounter with him at the hospital, his SMS which she still had on her phone and then, the final disastrous evening at the coffee shop. For the umpteenth time, Sandhya saw a row of frownies form in her mind's eye and she sighed. Clearly, she had a HUUUGE crush on Akshi and no chance of getting him.

He was super cute, for sure. All the girls freaked when they spotted him. But it wasn't just about being cute. There was something more to Akshi than just his good looks. He had a kind expression and a twinkle in his eyes. What a combination – IRRESISTIBLE!

Sandhya was sure he had a great sense of humour as well. Only, she'd never get to find out! Akshi probably thought she was a real klutz. And chances of his actually having a long conversation with her were remote. Especially at the social, when he'd be mobbed by other, far prettier girls, without butter fingers, with better figures, cooler clothes. And of course, less dumb names!

What if he and all those others found out her 'real' name? Sandhya – what a name! How could Mom have called her that? And Dad, too. Why couldn't her parents have been a little more sensitive? They should have realised she was a young girl of the twenty-first century. She wanted a modern name. And Mom had not named Bhaiya after a God. She could've called him Vishnu. Or Shiva. Neither was Pia named in such an old-fashioned way. Why her?

Sandhya had overheard Nani talking about her birth. She'd heard Nani say, "Poor Anu – what a tough time she had with this one. What a strenuous pregnancy. Anyway, I was sure my vow would see her through the worst. My prayers were answered – thank God. And we got our own little Sandhya, just as I had promised Lord Ganesh. I'd prayed and prayed. I'd said, 'Dear, dear Ganpati *Deva*, for years I've prayed to you with all my heart and asked for nothing. With your grace, I've got all that I need. But now, I want you to help my daughter through her difficult time. She needs your support. Let her have a safe delivery.' And since she was born late in the evening, we called her Sandhya."

So, Sandhya it had been – a name she didn't like. But was stuck with for sentimental reasons. Some old aunties and uncles liked it. And told her so.

"What a classical name! So charming! So old-fashioned! Just lovely!" they'd say, shaking their head in approval. Sandhya would smile back. But in her heart, she'd be seething.

"As if it was my fault Mom had a hard time. At least she should've thought how I would feel being called Sandhya in today's day and age. Did anyone think of me and my views?"

So it was decided that though Sandhya would remain her "official" name, she would be called "Shona". Why "Shona"? Because it was the pet name given to her by a Bengali neighbour, who'd explained, "In Kolkata, we all have two names – the one on the birth certificate and the "dak naam" or a pet name used by the family with affection. Shona sounds nice and suits her." But Sandhya it was that stuck.

Sandhya practised new signatures every week. Sometimes she called herself Shakira or Priyanka. At other times, she experimented with the names of her favourite film stars. She called herself Kareena for two weeks. Then switched to Preity.

"What about Pooja or Piali or Punita?" her friends recommended. Sandhya was adamant. "Anything but... suggest some foreign names. I like Aaliya or Fiona or Taslima or Nafisa or Carrie or Zeta. Something that makes me sound different, mysterious. Nobody will be interested in knowing a Sandhya."

And that had become her ongoing problem.

It didn't help at all that Ma lectured her constantly about accepting her given name. "Come on... don't be like this. Learn to accept it. Learn to love it. Only then will you be able to love and accept yourself properly. It's a beautiful name."

But now, back to earth. What about her plan?

Chapter Sixteen

A Dark Plan

Sandhya's plan was simple. She would call up the *pujari* and pretend to be her mother. She would tell him that due to an emergency operation on Nana, the puja date would have to be shifted. She would muffle her voice with a handkerchief placed over the mouthpiece. She'd say a fresh date would be given soon. Then she'd go to her mother and tell her just the opposite – that the *pujari* had phoned to cancel the puja since he had to rush to his village to attend to a sick relative. Why would her mother not believe the story? She would, right?

Sandhya felt terrible about lying. But she had to. It was that or missing the most important day in her life – the one every girl in her school waited for. The thought that the plan might backfire did not occur to her at all. Sandhya went over the phone call she would make to the *pujari* the next morning.

It was time to do a deal with the moon. Just like Nani had done with Ganpati *Deva*. Sandhya wanted to convince Chandamama to help her through the current crisis. If he'd do that, she in turn would promise never to lie to Mom again. If Chandamama stood by her this one time, she would be the "best-est" child ever. No fibbing. No bunking. And no... no... oh God! She couldn't get herself to even say those awful words. Sandhya buried her face in her hands and cried big fat tears. She'd never felt this miserable before. How could she have done that to Mom, Dad, her family? What sort of an example was she setting for Pia? How would Pia ever look up to her Didi now?

Chapter Seventeen

A Dreadful Nightmare

That night, Sandhya had a dream, a really strange one. Sandhya was a hard-core "dreamer" in any case. Even a light afternoon nap during summer holidays meant dreams galore – colourful, vivid and fantasy-filled. That was Sandhya's inner landscape since her early childhood. But these days, ever since the ... the... incident, her dreams had taken on a dark and sinister turn. Instead of amazing adventures in exotic destinations (Istanbul! Rio! Shanghai!), Sandhya dreamt of shadowy figures trailing her in a dense and dark forest. Horned, winged beasts swooped down, claws extended, to lift her up and away into the great unknown.

The sound effects were equally scary – deep growls, low roars and muted screams. If Sandhya tried to cry out she felt cold, clammy fingers tightening around her neck. Of course, it was no use trying to seek comfort from Pia by waking her up. Pia would only protest by yelling, "Ma-a-a... look at what Didi is doing to me..."

Sandhya knew she had to deal with the demons herself. But how very hard it was! Everything had taken on a sinister appearance, even the beautiful gulmohur tree she so loved, right outside her bedroom window. Sometimes, when Sandhya awoke at night in a cold sweat, the branches resembled threatening arms with extra long hands and nails. She thought she heard voices and whispers, and the leaves rustled in the breeze. Sometimes Sandhya imagined she saw figures lurking around the higher branches mocking her, ready to pounce if she moved even a bit in her damp-with-sweat bed.

Sandhya was sure she heard muffled laughter, as she lay frozen with fear, unable to tell anybody, even Mom, about the creatures who were coming in through the closed windows to punish her for what she'd done. During those agonising nights of lying awake, waiting for sunrise, Sandhya would recite the Gayatri Mantra taught to her by Mom. Somehow, it gave her enormous strength and confidence each time she repeated it. Gradually, her pulse rate would come back to normal, her dry throat would cease to be parched, and Sandhya would look towards the tiny silver image of Ganpati by her bedside and feel better. It was a feeling that didn't always sustain her though, and the restlessness would continue through her troubled day.

Tonight was no better. If anything, it was worse. Sandhya dreamt she was trapped in a tiny room underground. It was so constricted, she could barely move her limbs. Without water or food, she could hear her stomach rumble. There was a persistent knocking on the door, but, of course, Sandhya was paralysed with fear and unable to even crawl forward in that tiny, dark and dingy cell.

"We have come for you," unseen people kept repeating, as Sandhya prayed and prayed. The knocking grew louder, as Sandhya's heart pounded and leapt into her mouth. She felt gagged... suffocating as the cell itself began to shrink, with the walls closing in on her. Now, she was trapped in a tiny box, doubled up in a foetus-like position. The voices and knocking persisted. But a very bright light was shining on her face, blinding her.

Beyond the light, she could see the figure of a tall,

slim and graceful woman whose arms were raised. She was dressed in translucent silken robes, with long hair streaming down her back. She beckoned to Sandhya, who, while desiring to rush into her arms (maybe she was an angel on a mission to save her?), was unable to do so, since all movements were now totally frozen.

"Help me!"

Nothing emerged from her throat, except an incoherent, hoarse whisper. The light was still blinding. But the chorus of voices had risen to sound like a roar that could deafen her if it didn't stop. The woman in white was receding gradually, as if floating away into space. The light was fading too, and the chorus had turned down its volume to acceptable decibel levels. Sandhya's heart was not thudding any more. But she was shivering uncontrollably. The box in which she'd been trapped had suddenly expanded and was now a gigantic hall, with glittering chandeliers. Sandhya was placed right at the centre, but over a slab of ice.

She was minus clothes and her mouth was taped. She could barely move her neck, but could hear those strange voices, as if they were coming at her from several different directions simultaneously. Sandhya felt deep shame at her own nakedness. But her hands were tied behind her back, and her feet were bound. The chandelier had started to move in gradually increasing circles. She could hear the tinkling of the dangling crystal. But she was also afraid the massive chandelier would come crashing down on her and crush her.

The hall was now the size of a field. The ice slab had been replaced by a platform that was horribly spiked. Sandhya was dressed in rags. The person staring down at her was a cross between her school principal and the person she'd once spotted at a traffic light, who'd startled her by knocking aggressively on the car window to ask for alms. Sandhya squeezed her eyes shut to block out the awful sight. But someone was prying her eyelids open and saying something in a child's voice.

"Wake up Didi... Please. You are disturbing me again. You and your crazy, stupid dreams. Why don't you just sleep under your bed or something? That way you can dream away and not wake me up with your silly mumbling. Wait till I complain to Mom."

Sandhya was very relieved to escape her nightmare. She turned gratefully to Pia and hugged her. Pia struggled out of her grasp and said, "Yuck! Puh-leeze. What's wrong with you? Go hug a tree or something."

Sandhya smiled to herself. In a strange way the series of nightmares had pushed her towards a solution. No, she wouldn't lie to anybody. And she definitely wouldn't make that phone call to the *pujari*. Somewhere, she knew she'd found the right route to her mother's heart.... and salvation! But would Mom understand? Really, really understand??

Chapter Eighteen

Confessions Galore

More than two weeks had passed since that nightmare. Bhaiya's "confession" had been simple and straightforward. He'd told Mom and Dad the truth right after a rather strained dinner.

"Yes, I have smoked a few times – and those cigarette butts in the room are mine. But, I want you to know, I'm not a regular smoker. And never will become one. I smoke when my friends smoke. Stupid reason – but there it is. I'm young. I feel tempted. I want to belong. Again, that's not reason enough. But I want to make a promise tonight – that I will try my very best to quit. I'm aware smoking is bad for me. I know how strongly you guys feel about it. I don't want to hurt your feelings. Above all, I don't want to lose your trust. So... help me. But if I occasionally slip up – forgive me, too."

Mom had spontaneously gone up to Bhaiya and hugged him. "Thank you for being honest," she'd said with tears in her eyes.

Dad had been less forthcoming. He'd sat really, really quietly, obviously in deep thought. Finally, he'd left the room saying, "This is something I need to chew on."

Mom had hastily signalled to Bhaiya, indicating he leave the room. She needed time with Dad to sort it out between themselves. The girls had slipped away as well and reassembled on Bhaiya's comfy bed.

"Sorry kids," Bhaiya had said. "I know this is a tough one. But I swear I'm going to try really really hard. It's a terrible habit. And I want you both to know that I don't think it's "cool" to smoke. It is anything but! It's actually a disgusting habit... but I know I can do it – I can quit. And I'm going to."

Sandhya nodded sympathetically, while Pia fidgeted. "No big deal, Bhaiya... Binu from my class smokes too... and so do Tina and Natasha."

When Sandhya had heard that, she screamed,

'WHAT ?" so loudly, Mom had come running into the room. Bhaiya had frozen, mid-sentence, himself.

"Rubbish! Don't make up such silly stories," Sandhya had snapped.

"Don't believe me – I don't care. Or phone Payal and ask her yourself – she's seen them smoking. Swear. Why would I make it up?"

Bhaiya had made Pia sit down on his bean bag, while Mom had stood towering over her.

"You must be kidding," Bhaiya had stuttered. "Smoking? At this age? Oh man – what's going on?"

Mom had a worried frown creasing her brow. "This is very troubling. Very. Pia, are you sure? These children are so young – kids! Do their parents know? Does the school? And how do they get their hands on cigarettes?"

Pia smiled, "What's tough about that? They steal money... or they steal cigarettes. Their parents smoke – yes – mom and dad. And they don't count how many cigarettes there are in their pockets every day. It's so easy!"

At that unfortunate moment, in walked Dad.

"Did I hear right?" Dad asked as the family froze.

His expression was stern and his back stiffer than usual. Mom widened her eyes, so Sandhya alone could see. It was their little signal that meant, "Dad's had a rough day...don't harrass him."

Sandhya intervened quickly to say, "Nothing... nothing... Da... chill out... just some silly school problem."

Suddenly, Dad broke into loud laughter. He laughed so hard, he had to clutch his sides.

Mom exchanged quick looks with the children as if to say, "Has he lost it? Weird!!"

Dad sat down on Bhaiya's bed and continued to chortle.

Finally, he said, "Look... you guys seem to believe I was born an old man! I know what you think – that I'm a stuffy chartered accountant whose only interest is balance sheets. I know you find me boring and old-fashioned. I know you'll never believe me when I say, 'Hey... guess what? I was also your age once upon a time. And that was not centuries ago.' I may appear like a dinosaur to you, but you know something? I know exactly what you're talking about."

Mom smiled nervously and said with a small laugh, "If you know, then why are you laughing so much? It's a pretty serious subject!"

Dad shrugged. "That's what my parents said too. I can hear their voices clearly. 'Dev Beta, why are you smoking? It is bad for health. We are shocked and hurt. The neighbours have been talking that you're getting out of control. They see you smoking under the banyan tree before coming home. Beta, this is not good. Think of your future. Smoking is harmful, Beta. Nobody smokes in this family. Where did you pick up such a dirty habit? It's the bad company you keep.'"

Dad looked around at them with a lop-sided, uncharacteristic grin on his face. "Familiar words? You've heard them from both of us, right? Bet you could never have imagined your dad being scolded or lectured to by your dada-dadi, right? Bet you think I was a studious good-goody, who never disobeyed his parents, right? Bet you also thought I was the biggest nerd you'd ever seen! It's okay.

"But the truth is, I was a wild child. I did all sorts of crazy, stupid things when I was your age. I wanted to give up school and start a rock band. I bunked classes. Once, I even left home "forever"; I got as for as Nashik, panicked and took a train back to Mumbai. Yes my dear, I considered myself a rebel.

"I refused to shave or cut my hair; my parents couldn't bear to look at me! I played the drums all night long. I played the tabla too. I loved both Ravi Shankar and the Beatles. Couldn't decide what to do. That was the time I tried everything – smoking, drinking, even *ganja*... don't look so shocked! I'm telling you so you know the whole truth."

Bhaiya had tears clouding his eyes as he spontaneously leaned across to hug his father. "Dad... I love you. And thanks for sharing this with us – it means so much. It means you trust us to understand your past... sorry if we made you feel like a nerd."

Pia started to giggle just then, as Sandhya glared. It was Mom who smiled broadly and went across to where Dad was sitting.

"How about that? The secret is out now. Come on Dev, get those drums. And your old jeans. Let's bring out those Ravi Shankar records and let's sing *Strawberry Fields Forever.*"

Dad joined in the laughter, while Sandhya asked, "Isn't Ravi Shankar Norah Jones's dad?"

Pia said, "Who is Norah Jones?"

"She's Anoushka's half-sister – don't you know anything?"

Bhaiya started looking through his CD rack,

obviously searching for something special.

"There!" he said triumphantly, "I knew I had it somewhere." Waving a CD around and dancing a little jig, he refused to say which one it was. "Listen... just listen."

And the first few bars of *Norwegian Woods*, with the melodious strains of a sitar, filled the room. Sandhya watched her parents sing the song in unison; they knew every line, every word. Only Pia looked "out of it" and totally bored.

"Eeew! I think I'll go and play at Payal's house."

The magical spell was finally broken when Bhaiya's cell phone rang. It was his badminton buddy wondering whether he was going to make the game.

"On my way," Sid said hastily, grabbing his kit.

Just before he left Dad stopped him at the door and said, "Son, we need to talk man-to-man one of these days. I want to tell you how foolish I was about cigarettes. I thought I was proving something to my parents by sticking that silly weed into my mouth and puffing away. Do you know what it cost me? My decathlon medal! I didn't have the stamina to compete or complete the events the way I once could have.

"It was a big blow to me, to my self-esteem. My losing the championship that year affected everything – including my admission. I lost my then-girlfriend as well – she preferred the winner! So... think about what I've just told you. Kids go through different phases. Boys your age want to show how tough and grown-up they are. But smoking and drinking only pull you down. Today, your badminton game is good enough for you to be in the team. Tomorrow, if your stamina drops, you'll be dropped too. Is it worth it?"

Sid looked down at his new keds. He suddenly felt like the little boy who used to ride behind his dad on a motorcycle, hanging on for dear life, as his father wove his way expertly through peak hour traffic, making it to Sid's school seconds before the bell rang. How long ago that seemed! And yet, today as he spoke to him in a low steady voice, Sid knew that Dad's entire "act" had been designed to drive the message home.

He hugged his father warmly and said in a voice gruff with emotion, "Dad... I want you to know I have understood. I am going to try hard and sincerely to do what is right for me and for all of us. That's a sure thing Dad, believe me. I need to do one hell of a lot of deep thinking about stuff I've refused to deal with. Will tell you about it some other time... lunch next week?"

Dev nodded silently. He was glad he'd taken the route he had. Had he thundered and shouted, as the kids had probably expected him to, the effect would've been totally different. The kids would've listened, but not really "heard". Something in him had told him not to be the conventional 'Angry Father' reprimanding his children for their 'bad behaviour'. On the spur of the moment, he had decided to reveal aspects of his life that very few people (including his wife, Anu) knew too much about. Dev felt lighter and also reassured. As if a weight had somehow dropped off his shoulders. And the love of those he loved the most, was reinforced in a way that he would cherish forever.

Sandhya could feel her heart pounding. It was a do-or-die, now-or-never moment. If she let it go, it would be gone forever. Intuitively, instinctively, she just knew that this was the right time, the best time. The 'secret' that had been consuming her for so long, couldn't stay buried deep within for another second. She would confess! She took a deep breath...

Chapter Nineteen

Now Or Never!

Sandhya said a quick, silent prayer, squeezed her eyes shut, and blurted it out in one go, "Mom, Dad... Wait, I have something to confess, too... I lied."

Dev who was on his way out of the room, stopped in his tracks and stared at his daughter quizzically.

Bhaiya stopped and turned back, fidgeting with his belt buckle (an old habit that indicated he was thinking), and looked at his sister with an expression she hadn't seen before. Pia was about to interrupt when Anu put an arm around her and said, "Sssh... let Didi speak. She wants to tell us something."

Sandhya's eyes were swimming with tears, her

throat was parched, her tongue heavy.

She tried to speak, but what emerged was a hoarse whisper.

"Promise you won't hate me," she finally managed to say.

"Please Ma, please Dad... do anything... say anything... but don't hate me. I know I've done something terrible... I am so ashamed... but I'll make it up to all of you... just don't hate me, that's all."

Dev was the first to speak.

"You are our child – we can never hate you, Beta. We may get very angry with you. But hate? No parent hates a child, regardless of what happens. So... relax... don't be scared. Come here... sit down... breathe deeply... go on... take a long breath... now exhale slowly... sip a little water...your mouth is dry."

By now Anu had joined Dev and was stroking Sandhya's hair. There was a strange silence in the room, broken only by Pia's flip-flops making a whoosh-whoosh sound as she swung her legs from the side of the bed.

When Sandhya was slightly calmer, she said, "Please Mom... Dad... I need to go to the loo... be right back."

She rushed out and locked herself in the bathroom. Perched on the toilet seat, she prayed and prayed, "Please God... give me the strength to come out with the truth. Please God... whatever the punishment, I'll take it... but please, please, Ganpati *Deva*, don't let Mom and Dad stop trusting me, loving me..."

Suddenly she heard music... it was the Gayatri Mantra. The one she'd been taught by Ma when she was a little girl of eight. Sandhya wasn't sure where it was coming from. Perhaps a neighbour's radio... but the music was wafting softly, sweetly through the bathroom window... Sandhya felt soothed and comforted.

"It's a sign, God, isn't it? It is from you, right? And you're telling me not to worry... that it's okay... right? Thanks God... thanks a lot."

Sandhya went back to the room, where her family was waiting. She was walking taller, straighter and breathing normally. Her eyes were shining and her voice was back. She entered the room and said softly, "I did not appear for my Science exam in the finals. I've flunked Maths. And the report card says I might have to repeat the year. I lied that the report card had not yet been given out. I lied about how well I'd done. I lied that my class teacher was happy with me. In fact, this has been the worst year of my school life – and I'm so ashamed I lied about my failure."

Sandhya stopped abruptly. There. It was out. It was done. It was over. All she could do now was await her family's verdict. She was prepared for whatever lay ahead. She was no longer afraid, no longer panic-stricken. Now, her secret was also her family's. And she knew, Mom and Dad would deal with it in the best way.

It was Bhaiya who spoke first. He said to Sandhya, "Why did you do it? Why lie? And why did you flunk and bunk in the first place?"

Sandhya felt fresh tears smarting her eyes. Before she could answer, Pia piped in, "Didi flunked because she didn't study – simple. She was too busy on the phone!"

Sandhya glared at her but said nothing. Then she added softly, "And one more thing. I nearly cancelled the Satyanarayan Puja because I desperately wanted to go to the school social and it fell on the same day. I'd thought of a plan… I was going to phone the *pujari* and pretend to be Mom. But I didn't. I know it's a terrible thing… but… but I didn't want to miss the social at any cost. I know I'm a bad girl and you all will hate me forever."

Anu held out her arms and said, "Come here!"

Sandhya hadn't expected such a reaction from Mom – not Mom! She rushed gratefully into her mother's arms and sobbed. Anu kept repeating, "We'll talk about this later, when you are less upset. Right now, I want you to finish crying – don't stop the tears. After that, have a shower. Think carefully about the past year. And once you do that, write it down. Just simple points will do. Figure out where it went wrong. Why did you do what you did? Once you are clear, we'll be able to better understand the sequence of events that led to this problem."

Sandhya buried her face in the soft folds of her mother's *dupatta*. Wave upon wave of sheer relief swept over her. And yet even in that distraught state, Sandhya was aware that Dad had not uttered a word so far. And she was wondering why. It was not like him not to react and say what he felt – especially at a time like this. Sandhya jerked herself out of her mother's embrace, whirled around and faced her father.

"Dad!" she implored.

"Talk to me!

"Why aren't you saying something?

"Tell me what a bad, horrible girl I've been. Tell

me you won't give me pocket money for a year – no movies, no TV, no keds, no clothes, no holiday, no outings. No cell phone. It's cool. I'll accept it. But I beg of you, say something, I can't bear your silence." In her heart, Sandhya was hoping Mom and Dad would forgive her. But would they?

Chapter Twenty

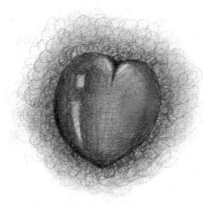

The Circle Of Love

Dev walked up to his weeping daughter. He caught her by her shoulders and held her at arm's length. "Look at me," he said, his voice steady and firm. "Look me in the eye."

Sandhya met her father's gaze nervously.

"What do you see?" Dev asked his daughter. "Rage? Hurt? Despair? Tell me – what do my eyes tell you? What is in them?"

Sandhya looked without averting her eyes from his or flinching. Finally, she shook her head and whispered, "I don't know Dad... I really don't... please... just slap me. I can deal with that. Punish me. Ground me... but..."

Dev interrupted her.

"Do you see love?" he demanded, shaking her by the shoulders. "Go on, look again... look deeply... do you see love?"

Sandhya burst into uncontrollable tears and nodded silently. Dev continued to hold her shoulders. "Look Sandhya... it is unfortunate that such a thing has happened. Later, we will get to the bottom of what went wrong academically this year. How come an honours student suddenly allowed her grades to slip? That's a separate question. The more important one according to me is why you didn't tell us. Why didn't you feel confident enough about your family to confide in even a single person? Why did you keep it all to yourself?

"That, to me, is the real issue. For Mom and I have always believed that our children had full faith in us. With faith comes trust. Have we let you down in some way? Those are questions we will ask ourselves. But for now, I need you to examine your own emotions. While you reply to Mom's questions about grades and bunking – a very serious lapse for a student, by the way – I want you to write another list which tells us all what it was that stopped you from involving us in your crisis. After all, that's when family counts. And if you didn't feel strongly enough that we'd stand by you and help you deal with the situation, then, we need to sit down and talk. And Mom and I need to ask ourselves, 'Have we failed Sandhya in some way?'

"Frankly, I don't care whether you skip a year – it's a loss, an important one, but you can always make it up. What I do care is that I want to win back your faith in all of us – each one of us. We are a unit, Sandhya, we must function like one. Mom and I are there for each one of you, no matter what. When you go wrong, we are there to get you back on track. At each step in your life, we are there – that is my message to you. And you should never forget it – WE ARE THERE. And always will be."

Dev left the room, after signalling to Anu to follow him.

Pia grinned at Sandhya.

"See – it was easy! No punishment, nothing. Lucky! Other parents lock up their children without food or water in a dark room for weeks and weeks."

Sid laughed and tousled Pia's hair. "Rubbish! Don't talk rot! I bet you're disappointed Didi didn't get a thrashing, right?"

And then he flung an arm around Sandhya. "Hey,

come on... let's go get something horrible... Burger? Ice cream? *Gola*? *Pav bhaji*? *Kulfi*?? There's nothing a burger can't fix. Come on... I'll take you for a spin... We'll talk – okay? But only if you want to."

Sandhya smiled. "Yeah, thanks Bhaiya. Good plan. Let's go. I could do with a disgusting, gooey, cheesy burger. Mom will get mad... but we will *patao* her somehow."

Bhaiya interjected with a wiggle of his eyebrows, "While we are on Mom... didn't Gauritai tell you the Satyanarayan Puja is off for the moment? Mom said we'd have it once Dada and Dadi were back from their holiday. See? If you'd only kept your big mouth shut about phoning the *pujari*, nobody would've known."

Sandhya nearly fainted on hearing that. Even the guilt over her confession to her parents about the proposed "puja delay plan" was swiftly forgotten.

All Sandhya could think of at that moment was, "Yeah! I can go to the social! Yeah! Yeah! Yeah!"

She jumped up and hugged Bhaiya tightly. "That's the best news... wow – I don't believe it... I can go... I can go... I can go."

Bhaiya laughed. "Sure you can... but right now, you'd better get out of here fast. I'm ravenous. Come on..."

Pia whined, "And me? What about me? I want an ice cream, too!"

And then Pia turned to Sandhya. "As if that Akshay will even notice whether you are at the social or not. Give up! He has a girlfriend. No... he has many girlfriends. Besides, you will be wearing that horrible denim skirt."

"Do we have to take the pest along? Why not include Zorro, too? And Gauritai?" Sandhya mock-pleaded.

Sid laughed. "You bet. We are family – remember?"

Coming Soon...

In the snappy happy Series

S's HEARTBREAK

Was it her 'uncool' dress? Her hair? Her nervous conversation? Or that clumsy moment when she'd made an ass of herself by tripping over her own feet?

Why had Akshi stopped talking to her? That too, when things were going so smoothly and she was sure this would last for ever and ever...

Sandhya knew she should never have listened to Mom and worn that dumb skirt. Nor should she have done her hair in that funny way.

"What a loser I am," she kept repeating over and over again.

Would Akshi forget that awful evening and get back with her? Or had he already moved on? Could Alisha be the new girl in Akshi's life??

Sandhya felt as if her heart had broken into a thousand pieces...

And there was just one way to heal it...